SHOCK

CHAD CARTWRIGHT

Book design by Chad Cartwright

Special thanks to family and friends,
Terry Handley, KJ Waters and Jeri Walker.

ISBN: 978-0-9975471-0-8 (1st edition paperback)
ISBN: 978-0-9975471-2-2 (1st edition ebook)

The Llano Life

My mother and father were both born and raised in Lubbock, Texas. My father graduated from high school at the height of the Vietnam conflict, as it was classified. War was never declared but it was definitely a war.

Well, Lubbock is just a big small town and my father got wind he was going to be drafted. He chose to enlist in the Navy before being drafted. Why would a landlocked West Texan choose the Navy? I have no idea. Perhaps, he thought it would be safer on a ship as the North Vietnamese were not known for their naval armada. I don't know. I never asked.

He was soon on a train to San Diego, California and was stationed at Camp Pendleton. He returned to Lubbock after boot camp and married my mother. They drove his '57 Chevy to Ruidoso, New Mexico where they spent their honeymoon and then continued the drive to San Diego. I was born nine months later.

My father became a Navy Corpsman. He was never on a ship but he did get a couple of plane rides to Vietnam. He served two tours. My mother said he wasn't the same after he came back to "The World" after being "In country". "The World" was life back in the states. "In country" was fighting in Vietnam.

She said the second tour had a dramatic impact on him. She thinks it was because between tours he was assigned to the surgery department at the camp hospital. Injured soldiers who were no longer able to fight but were medically stable enough to travel were flown to Camp Pendleton for rehabilitation and further surgeries if necessary.

At first, my father would come home and tell my mother stories about the wounded veterans. Those without legs made fun of those without arms who made fun of those with colostomies who made fun of those who were blind and so on. There was no pity in the recovery ward. These were bitter battle-hardened men whose country did not appreciate their physical, mental and emotional sacrifice.

He soon stopped talking about anything that happened at the hospital. My mother would ask him how his day was and she would get the generic "Fine." She knew he had seen and been a part of horrible things in Vietnam. He told her very little about his first tour and even less about the second. The little he told her when he got back stateside was enough for my mother to get a glimpse of his experience in the war.

She thinks his seeing the physical carnage at the hospital every day finally got to him. One day, she overheard him talking to himself. She couldn't make all of it out but she distinctly heard him say, "What shape will I come home in?...if I come home."

The day before he left on his second tour, he found out the best man at his wedding, his best friend, was dead. His best friend just started his second tour. He didn't make it a week after he left "The World" and was back "In country." My father was devastated and disillusioned. He actually considered going AWOL. He didn't think he was going to make it back alive. If, by some miracle, he did make it back alive, he was certain he'd be maimed for life.

My father didn't go AWOL. He got on a plane. My father was on a plane to Vietnam as the body of his best friend was on another plane headed to Camp Pendleton.

He did make it back alive but was forever a changed man. He was honorably discharged and despite often being on the front line during two tours he was never even grazed by a bullet or hit by shrapnel. It may have made him feel better if he had been injured. He certainly had survivor's guilt.

My parents always talk about how beautiful Southern California is. My mom reminisces about taking me to the beach and watching her blue-eyed son with bleach blond hair play in the sand. They talk about their perfect day, if there is such a thing.

As they tell it, they were at the beach one day, me playing in the sand, my mom soaking up some rays and my dad bodysurfing. My mother was watching me as she lay in the sun listening to KROQ on the radio. A weather report came on. It was snowing at the Palomar Observatory. My mom yelled at my dad who was standing in the surf looking for a good wave.

They grabbed me and threw our stuff in the back of my dad's '57 Chevy. They raced to our apartment, grabbed some clothes and drove 64 miles to the observatory. It had been a long time since they had seen snow. They rushed there to enjoy the snow before it melted and they also did it for me. That was the first time I had ever seen snow.

They didn't have any snow boots for me so they wrapped plastic bags around my shoes. My father set me down in the snow as my mother moved back a few feet from us. She knelt down to get a picture of my first time in the snow. I took one step and fell face first into the fresh powder. (I have managed to fall on my face many times since then.) My face plant was too fast for her to take a picture.

My mother said I fell in a patch of snow just deep enough for me to disappear completely. My father dug me out of the snow and turned me around. My face was covered with snow but he could see I was smiling from ear to ear and laughing. My father turned me around so my mother could see me and she took our picture. I was a happy little snowman. We spent the rest of the day playing in the snow.

In the midst of an unpopular war with only each other to depend on, a young child to look after and them being young themselves with an uncertain future, it must have been a very good day.

They couldn't afford to live in San Diego after my father left the service. My mother begged my father to stay but he knew they needed to move. The cost of living there then, as it is now, was sky high. My mother understood this but also realized as much as he loved the beach and Southern California, he needed to get away from Camp Pendleton and the war.

I was three years old when we moved to Lubbock. The city is located on the Llano Estacado, the largest mesa on the North American continent. Lubbock is flat, dusty and windy. Even in town, the occasional tumbleweed will attack you like it's a bowling ball and you're the last pin standing. Massive dust storms called haboobs periodically form on the plains of West Texas and will engulf the city. If a rainstorm happens to occur at the same time as a haboob, it will rain mud. I had the pleasure of experiencing this one day when walking home from school.

Lubbock is the hometown of Buddy Holly, Texas Tech University and prairie dogs. There is a statue of Buddy Holly downtown. I never realized how famous he was until I travelled out of the country. When I told some foreigners I was from Lubbock, almost all of them would say "Buddy Holly! I know where Lubbock, Texas is." There was a movie made about him starring Gary Busey as Buddy. (This was pre-crazy Busey.)

There used to be a Buddy Holly music festival every year. It was cancelled by a cease and desist order from his widow, Maria Elena Holly. She will not let anyone use his name or likeness without getting paid for it. The plaza where his statue is prominently displayed in front of the West Texas Walk of Fame was formally named the Buddy and Maria Elena Holly Plaza. She demanded her name be included.

Lubbock has the highest concentration per capita of churches and restaurants in the nation. Sex education isn't allowed in Lubbock schools. So, it also has the highest teen pregnancy rate in the state, second in the nation. Apparently, going to church, eating or screwing are the only things to do here.

The package sale of alcohol is prohibited within the city limits but bars and restaurants can serve alcohol (probably why there are so many restaurants). The only place you can buy booze is outside the city limits at "The Strip". The Strip is just a row of stores all selling beer, wine and liquor. It is literally across the street from the city limit sign. This is where you will find the majority of Lubbockites on a Friday night. There's always a traffic jam on Friday nights or whenever Tech plays.

Texas Tech University is an awesome place to go to school. You get a good education and it's a lot of fun. There are parties, plenty of bars and a lot of good-looking women. A statue of Will Rogers on his favorite horse, Soapsuds, is one of the most well-known landmarks on the campus. The Saddle Tramps, an all-male booster organization that supports men's athletics at Texas Tech, wrap Old Will and Soapsuds with red crepe paper for every home football game. According to legend, Soapsuds' posterior is pointed in the direction of one of our rivals, Texas A&M. Football games are a blast, especially if we beat A&M or

Texas at home. The goal posts have been torn down and carried across campus a time or two.

Lubbock has a habitat for prairie dogs in one of the parks cleverly named "Prairie Dog Town". There was a crazy old man who converted his van into a mobile prairie dog catcher. He lined the back of his van with old mattresses and made a supercharged vacuum to catch the rodents. He would connect a large hose to the vacuum and then shove the other end of the hose into one of the numerous holes leading to their underground parade of homes. He would turn on the vacuum and suction the unsuspecting varmints from their labyrinth into the hose.

The prairie dogs went for a mini-amusement park ride which ended with them slamming into and bouncing off of a mattress like a dull dart. He even painted a bull's-eye on the mattress. You could watch all of this through a window he installed on the side of the van. The prairie dogs were dazed for a bit but unharmed. It was pretty funny to watch.

Once he bagged his quota, he delivered them to the world famous Prairie Dog Town. The farmers and ranchers appreciated his work even if he was a weirdo. Most people in Lubbock are fairly normal though. You'll find the real crazies in the border towns. For some reason, the closer you live to Mexico the crazier you are.

Needless to say, Lubbock is a conservative town. The surrounding farmland is the largest producer of cotton in the world. The cotton grown on top of the soil and the oil residing deep below it have made many here very wealthy. Raising cattle is pretty lucrative as well.

My parents moved back to Lubbock so my dad could go to Tech. My dad is very smart. He worked full time on the night shift in the emergency room of the now defunct West Texas

Hospital. This hospital was in the worst part of town and had the busiest ER, especially on Friday and Saturday nights.

At the same time, he earned a Bachelor of Science degree in biology with a minor in chemistry and a 4.0 GPA. He applied and was accepted into medical school but decided to be a registered nurse instead. He told me he was tired of school and saw how much doctors worked. Instead of attending medical school, he decided he'd rather just work a shift and be with his family. That was good enough for him. I respect him for that.

By this time, my brother was born. On August 16, 1977, the day Elvis died, my brother was born. Reincarnated, I believe. Grant was the final addition to our family. He was named after my father's best friend.

We didn't have much of an extended family. Neither of my parents had siblings so there were no aunts, uncles or cousins to speak of. My maternal grandparents were killed in a car accident and my paternal grandmother died from breast cancer. Our only living relative was my grandfather, Friedrich Rousser.

He fascinated me. My grandfather was a World War II veteran, not an American soldier though. He was a German soldier on the Eastern Front. That's all I knew. He wouldn't talk about it and that just made me even more curious.

After the war, my grandparents immigrated to the United States. They travelled with numerous post-war German immigrants to Texas with the intent of making Fredericksburg their new home. Fredericksburg is located in the heart of the Texas hill country. It was founded in 1846 by a small group of German settlers and was named after Prince Frederick of Prussia. It is also the birthplace of Fleet Admiral Chester Nimitz. Ironically, this Admiral of German descent served as Commander in Chief of the United States Pacific Fleet during World War II.

My grandparents never made it to Fredericksburg though. They stopped in Lubbock and stayed. Perhaps, they decided to live in Lubbock because it sounded like Lubeck, a city in Germany. For whatever reason, they stayed and bought a small house in the neighborhood known as Tech Terrace located across the street from Texas Tech University.

The university is north of 19th Street and Tech Terrace is south. Like almost all of Lubbock's neighborhoods, Tech Terrace is a square grid of homes with streets running north and south and east and west. The streets running north and south are named in alphabetical order. The streets running east and west are in numerical order.

Tech Terrace is now a trendy and expensive place to live except along University Avenue. On the east side, where University Avenue runs, is where Tech students mainly live. On the west side of the neighborhood, where the park is, runs Indiana Avenue. This is where the old homes have been restored and the property values are considerably higher. My grandfather's house is in the middle. He lives east of rich and west of dicey. The neighborhood extends south to 34th Street.

My grandfather is a semi-retired electrician. He was his own boss and had no employees because no one could stand to work for him. My grandfather was a very hard worker and demanded that everything be done the right way, his way or the highway. He always had plenty of work though because he was the best electrician in town.

My grandfather was also the only babysitter I ever knew. The few times my parents needed someone to look after my brother and me, Grandpa Freddy would take care of us. That's what we called him but never to his face. Opa is the informal name for grandfather in German but we always had to call him by the more formal Grossvater.

He would take off work to babysit us if he needed to. That was the only time he ever took off work. He was a workaholic but he was always there for us. He was stern but was always teaching us something. His grandmother taught him Russian by only speaking Russian to him and he did the same thing with us except we learned to speak German. My father was raised in a bilingual household and my grandfather firmly believed we should be as well.

Grandpa Freddy would get so mad if we were not speaking German when he came over to our house. My mother didn't mind us speaking German but she didn't think it was that important. She joked that we were always talking about her when Dad, Grant and I would speak in German.

Salad Days

I must have been hard to deal with. My mother washed my mouth out with soap on numerous occasions. Spankings occurred often. I tried the book in the pants trick but that never works. A rectangular butt is a dead giveaway.

One time, I knew I was about to get spanked and had a not-so-bright idea. I ran into my room and found my pocket knife. My mother came in my room with the wooden spoon. I pulled my knife out and opened it. I pointed it at her and told her in no uncertain terms that I was not going to be spanked now or ever again! In the blink of an eye, that knife was out of my hand and in hers. She slowly closed it and put it in her pocket without saying a word. I then got the worst spanking of my life. Grant thought it was funny. I did not. I still don't. I never got my knife back either.

My brother was almost five years younger than me so naturally he got picked on quite a bit. I had a lot of help from my best friend, Theodore Barnes. Along with the standard physical and verbal abuse, we enjoyed messing with his head. One day, we convinced my brother that he was adopted. "I knew it! I knew I was different!" he cried as he ran to my mother. My mother then ran to me and spanked me with the wooden spoon again. And again, Ted was banished from our home.

11

We lived on the corner of a major street and our backyard was surrounded by a short fence. We had a trampoline and when we were jumping on it we were easily visible from the street. One day, Ted and I convinced Grant to jump on the trampoline naked. Why? Who knows? Kids do stupid things. We told him it would be cool or some nonsense.

My mother had been running errands and was on her way home. As she pulled into the turn lane of our busy street, she was greeted by the sight of her redheaded, fair-skinned and naked little boy bouncing up and down on the trampoline for all of Lubbock to see. He got the wooden spoon that time. For some reason, he didn't rat us out. Grant was a tough kid. I was book smart while he was athletic and street smart. Grant was the extrovert and I was the introvert. He always looked up to me. Unfortunately, I wasn't always a good example.

My parents were big believers in education. My mother wouldn't let me play after school until I got my homework done. It worked though. I always got straight A's.

My public education started at Maedgen Elementary School, home of the Mohawks. The Maedgen library is where I found my first history book. My reading class went to the library and we were told to pick a book to read. I found a book about Nazis. It had pictures of swastikas, Hitler and dead bodies. These were all things I had never seen before. I became engrossed in the book. Is this what my grandfather witnessed?

As I flipped through the last of the pictures, my teacher snatched the book from my hands. She admonished me for reading such a "horrid" book and made me check out *Where the Red Fern Grows* instead. After school, I snuck back into the library and "borrowed" the history book. I still read *Where the Red Fern Grows*. It made me cry.

Other than my early interest in World War II, I was a fairly normal kid. I was in Cubs Scouts and played baseball and soccer. Ted and I did everything together. He was the fat kid and I was the scrawny kid. We looked like the number 10 when we stood beside each other. His dad was a college baseball player and coached our little league baseball team.

As a kid, I couldn't understand why he was our coach because he could barely walk. I didn't know his dad had ALS (amyotrophic lateral sclerosis), otherwise known as Lou Gehrig's disease. He was drafted but didn't go to Vietnam because he was found to have abnormal reflexes and didn't pass the physical. The Lou Gehrig's wasn't diagnosed until later.

One of my favorite childhood memories involves Ted's mom and dad. They took us to Buffalo Springs Lake one summer weekend. Ted and I were hiking in the canyon looking for many of the small caves and Indian artifacts found there.

Unfortunately, we hiked right into a hornet nest. We ran away as fast as we could but it wasn't fast enough. We really pissed them off and they stung us like crazy. Their venom packs a punch. We found Ted's parents and they were mortified to see us in our sorry state. We were crying and covered with hornet stings. Ted's dad went into the bait and tackle shop and got a pouch of Red Man chewing tobacco. He started chewing and then putting the saliva-laden tobacco on our stings. It was a slow-going process for one person so Ted's mom started doing the same to speed things up a bit. Needless to say, Ted's mom had never chewed tobacco. It didn't take long for her to start violently vomiting. The comic relief Ted and I got from that was enough to make us forget about our hornet-induced misery.

I didn't excel at sports so I decided to try karate instead. I got to be pretty good at it and earned my black belt by the time I started junior high. I and almost all of my friends went to J.T.

Hutchinson Junior High School, home of the Rangers. It was an honor school. My friends' parents were strong proponents of education as well. Our parents made sure we were enrolled in all of the honor courses available.

The classes were tough but I managed to keep straight A's. I failed to make the football or basketball team though. My parents even paid for me to go to basketball camp one summer. I got the most improved award which just meant I didn't suck as much as when I got there. So, I was put on the wrestling team since there was no one for the 100-110 pound weight class. I might have weighed 100 pounds fully dressed and soaking wet with a full bladder.

Our wrestling coach was old school. Coach Winston chomped on a cigar and harassed us to no end. He was more of a drill sergeant than a coach. The slowest runner on the wrestling team was a black kid. Coach would yell at him as we ran laps.

"Leroy! How the hell does a black kid run slower than every white boy on this team?! From now on you are to be known as the honorary white boy!"

One of our teammates had the unfortunate surname of Snodgrass which Coach converted to Boogerweed. One day, Coach Winston did not appreciate Boogerweed's wrestling form.

"Boogerweed! That's not how you do a takedown!"

Coach decided to use Boogerweed as a test subject to demonstrate the proper technique for a blast double takedown. In this type of takedown, the attacking wrestler uses his head to push his opponent's body out of position while grabbing both legs behind the knees. It's basically tackling your opponent. So, after watching Coach Winston drive Boogerweed into the mat, I made sure my takedowns were executed perfectly. I didn't want a private lesson.

I experienced a lot of my firsts in junior high. My first kiss, my first handful of boob, my first drunk and my first joint were all experienced during those formative years. Then it was on to Lubbock High School, home of the Westerners.

Buddy Holly went to Lubbock High School. He didn't have a choice as it was the only high school at the time. My life experiences and education grew exponentially during those years. Lubbock High also offered honor courses which naturally I was enrolled in.

I managed to become a decent wrestler and even got third place in city but I only needed one semester of physical education to graduate so I decided to take a semester of gymnastics instead of continuing my wrestling career. I packed on the pounds and was in the 110-120 pound weight class the last year I wrestled. It didn't really break my heart to retire as we went from t-shirt and shorts to wrestling in the traditional wrestling singlet. The singlet was not a good look for me. A scrawny white boy with no muscle tone and a little dick protruding from his size small singlet isn't a pretty sight. It turned out I should have stuck with wrestling.

Gymnastics wasn't easy. I racked myself numerous times on the pommel horse but my best routine was the vault. On my very first attempt, I vaulted myself straight in the air. I landed spread-eagle on the vault simultaneously racking myself and face-planting. I lay there for a brief moment before sliding off the side of the vault. The gym was eerily quiet during my routine. As soon as I hit the ground, the room erupted in laughter. I had no idea gymnastics could cause so much damage to a scrotum. It's amazing my crotch survived that semester.

I met my first drug dealer in gymnastics as well. He was crazy. He would drop acid before class and bounce around on the mat doing front and back flips. I never had the balls to do something like that. I smoked pot at lunch a few times but that's about it. It did make algebra more interesting.

Lubbock High was a wild place. It was like *Fast Times at Ridgemont High*. There really weren't distinct groups though. Rich, poor, athletic, preppy or punk - It didn't matter. Everyone mingled together. There was one distinction though. It was between the students who lived in the school district and those who transferred there for the honor courses. That was noticeable. The honor course classrooms were on the west side of the school and the regular classes were on the east side of the school. The only time we went to the east side of the school was to buy beer at lunch.

There was a guy with a van (no relation to the prairie dog catcher) who sold beer. He was an entrepreneur really. There was a need in the market and he met it. He would pull up next to the school in his A-Team van and slide open the door. He had a modestly iced keg in the van and would sell a red solo cup full of rodeo cold beer for a dollar.

Fights were a regular, if not a weekly, occurrence. Inevitably, they would take place in the middle of the main hallway which is where the trophy case is conveniently located. The defeated opponent was commonly thrown into the trophy case.

The most violent fight I ever saw was between two male gymnasts. The funniest and most painful to watch were the girl fights. Copious amounts of Aquanet were used by high school girls in the late 80's. Aquanet is an industrial strength hair spray. It can make hair do anything but it makes the hair very stiff and apparently easy to grab during a fight. When slapping and scratching gave way to hair pulling, it was not a pretty sight. My personal favorite was the time Jose Briones got in a fight with two girls. He managed to get both of them in headlocks and prayed one of the teachers would break up the fight before they managed to get loose and tear him apart.

There was a split school schedule. Monday through Thursday we had honor classes but Friday was different. School was from 8:00 am to noon. We had "Friday Classes". These were classes like Film Appreciation, Bachelor Cooking, Photography, etc. They were just participatory classes, no grades. As you can imagine, there was a lot of tomfoolery, hijinks and shenanigans on Fridays. Now, as I mentioned earlier, there is no sex education in Lubbock schools. This was evident by the number of girls in school who were mothers. Fridays being our casual day, the teenage mothers would bring their kids to school with them. It was like show and tell with babies. One Friday, the principal had enough of it and got on the loudspeaker.

"Attention. Attention. Students are NOT allowed to bring their children to school. Please stop bringing your children to school. Thank you."

It was basically sex, drugs and rock and roll.

Outside of school, there were plenty of house parties. The location just depended on whose parents were out of town that particular weekend. If we wanted to get out of town, we'd drive to Lincoln National Forest just outside of Carlsbad, New Mexico. We'd get a couple cases of beer and drive into the mountains on the other side of Carlsbad Caverns. There are a bunch of caves in the mountains but nothing as big as Carlsbad Caverns. We would explore caves during the day and drink beer at night. We got carried away with our campfires a few times. They easily turned into bonfires and we almost burned down Smokey's forest one night.

In the summers, we would go backpacking in Colorado with my friend Chuck's church group. They were Church of Christ. If you're not familiar with Church of Christers, they're...well, they're a bit different. No cussing, no smoking, no drinking and definitely no musical instruments. For some reason, their music had to be acapella. Evidently, instruments are tools of the devil.

The trips were awesome though. I didn't understand the people but I loved the mountains. We'd leave Lubbock about 4:00 am, have lunch in Santa Fe and arrive in Durango that evening. We'd camp for the night and the next morning we'd take the train from Durango north towards Silverton. The train would stop halfway and let us off. We'd backpack for a couple of weeks and then catch the train back to Durango. We rode back in the open air cars. We didn't smell very good after a fortnight in the Weminuche Wilderness.

Chuck, Ted and I spelled bad news for the CoCers (Church of Christers). Chuck was the best skateboarder in town. He was also the first kid in town to get a mohawk. Chuck cussed, smoked, drank and listened to punk music. This is not a good recipe for a young Church of Christ gentleman. We all thought we were so punk rock at the time. We couldn't listen to enough of the Misfits, Black Flag, Minor Threat, Social Distortion, the Sex Pistols, the Clash, etc.

There were always goober kids on the trips. A lot of them were homeschooled and had never been backpacking before or even camping for that matter. They were easy pickins for a trio of punk rockers.

One kid earned the nickname "Cutter" because he almost cut his thumb off with his Swiss Army pocket knife the very first day. Then there was the "Kool-Aid Man." One of the homeschoolers, Jed, loved Kool-Aid. He had never been backpacking before and didn't have the foresight to bring some with him. Chuck also enjoyed his Kool-Aid and brought plenty of packets with him. Jed had been begging Chuck to give him some. Chuck finally agreed to but only if Jed swam across the lake we hiked to that day. Now, lake water in the mountains of Colorado is very cold. Jed was not fit but he did have natural insulation. It wasn't a pretty sight but Jed stripped down to his underwear and swam across that lake. It was over a half-mile swim. He REALLY liked Kool-Aid. Jed wasn't too bright though. Chuck invited him to play poker with him that night. Jed lost the packet of Kool-Aid back to Chuck in the poker game.

The most memorable nickname came about from going on Solo. Solo was when the youth on the trip had to fast by themselves for 24 hours. We were allowed a bottle of water, a sleeping bag, a sleeping pad and a plastic sheet to make a shelter out of. We had to find a secluded spot to establish our own campsite and were not allowed to leave our campsite for 24 hours before returning to the main campsite. I'm still not sure what the purpose of this was. Perhaps it was simply supposed to show us if we had faith in God, we could rely on him to get us through the boredom and hunger.

One year, a Church of Christ group from Tennessee joined us on our annual backpacking trip. The goober kid that year was one of the Tennesseans. His name was Marshall. Marshall was fat and lazy. Ted was fat and I was scrawny but we did our best to keep up with the group. Marshall made no effort at all.

On the evening Solo was to begin, we were gathering our minimal belongings and preparing to venture into the woods on our own. There wasn't much to carry so most people just threw their stuff under their arms and took off in their own direction. I noticed Marshall was carrying a large black plastic bag over his shoulder. I was looking at him thinking that was odd when Chuck's older brother, Brian, stopped him. (We meanly referred to Chuck's brother as Brain but he wasn't stupid. We were just being ornery.)

"What's in the bag?"

"Huh?"

"The big black bag over your shoulder, WHAT's in it?"

"Nothin'."

"Nothin', huh? Open it."

Marshall dropped the bag off of his shoulder and opened it for Brian to look inside. What was inside? Marshmallows. Marshall had come prepared for Solo. The big black plastic bag was full of them. It was not very original but Marshall earned a new Delta Tau Chi nickname that day. For the rest of the trip, he was known as "Marshallmallow."

Backpacking, spelunking, partying and school was the majority of my life at that time, good times. The honor classes at Lubbock High were very hard. They prepared me well for college. In fact, I first thought about becoming a pharmacist after taking Chemistry 101 at Lubbock High. I thought it would be interesting to learn how drugs work. It seemed appropriate given the environment I received my education in. After graduating from Lubbock High, I enrolled at Texas Tech University.

Going South

Ted and I were roommates at Tech. I studied and he joined a fraternity. I had the privilege of partying with them once Ted completed his initiation. I felt like an honorary member. I doubt many of them would remember me because the only time I saw most of them were at parties. They enjoyed themselves.

I went to Tech for two years and completed my pre-pharmacy courses. Tech didn't have a pharmacy school at the time. The nearest school was at the University of Texas in Austin. I applied and was accepted. So, I packed my bags and headed south. Austin is the capital of Texas as well as the most liberal city and the most expensive place to live in Texas. I had no idea where I was going to live. Luckily, one of my friends from Lubbock lived there. His name is Robert Patterson. Robby just kicked his roommate out when I got into town so now I had a place to live.

Robby is not a partier. He is…eccentric. He looks like River Phoenix. All of the girls in school thought he was hot but he only dated foreign exchange students for some reason. He is very cheap and never loans anyone money. Robby refused to give Ted some loose change when we were playing quarter poker one night - unbelievably cheap.

He is also a teetotaler which is a far cry from my cohorts at Tech. Robby is crazy in his own way. I met him at Hutch and from day one I knew he was different. The first thing I remember about

Robby was when he told me he was an atheist. I was shocked by the notion of there not being a God. He made everybody think.

He was also a bit of a pyromaniac. Beginning in junior high, he sponsored his own book burning at the end of every school year. A block away from his house, there was an empty lot. In the center of the lot, he dug a pit. On the last day of school, he would invite everyone to his annual book burning and burn our school books. This tradition continued through high school.

One day, he caught the loop on fire. Loop 289 ran beside his parent's house. He was shooting bottle rockets at cars as they drove along the loop. The drought stricken grass between the lanes of the loop caught fire from a rocket that missed a car. Robby knew he had gone too far and ran to the fire hoping to extinguish it. It was too late though. The rest of us (now accomplices) watched him in disbelief.

We quickly got inside his parent's house. After giving up on the fire, Robby sprinted into the house as well. His shoes smelt of burnt rubber. When his father asked what the smell was, the quick thinking Robby said he burnt some toast. Why would someone make toast mid-afternoon? His dad didn't question it though. We then heard the fire trucks.

There was also one of the few lakes in Lubbock behind his house. He would catch fish and put waterproof fireworks in their mouths. He would then light the fuse, throw the fish back into the lake and wait for the fountain of water to erupt.

He never made it to any of the New Year's Eve parties. Robby was always on probation and couldn't be out past 10:00 pm. I take that back. He did sneak out of his parent's house for one New Year's Eve party.

He got to know the juvenile detention center very well. Robby had a knack for being at the wrong place at the wrong time with the wrong people. I know he just did it for the thrill. After he turned 18 and his juvenile records were expunged, he never got in trouble again. Robby was too smart.

Above all else, Robby was brilliant. He got a full ride scholarship to the University of Texas and was studying electrical engineering. He was also pre-med with a 4.0 GPA.

Pharmacy school was hard. I'm smart but I had to study. Robby never studied. He continued to date foreign exchange students whereas I only got laid once in a blue moon. His crazy ideas were the best thing about living with Robby. Now that we were living together in Austin, we would take off on all kinds of crazy road trips.

Big Bend was one of our favorite destinations. There is absolutely NOTHING in the Big Bend area of Texas and that is what makes it so awesome. At night in the high desert of West Texas, the stars are unbelievably clear. The nights there are darker than anywhere else in the country. That's why there is a state-of-the-art observatory there. In the Davis Mountains, you will find the McDonald Observatory. It's a research facility of the University of Texas. It is amazing how clearly you can see the heavens from there.

We loved hanging out in oddball West Texas towns like Marfa, Terlingua and Lajitas. Marfa is located between the Davis Mountains and Big Bend. It used to be a sleepy little town. Now it's turned into an art mecca. For some reason, more and more artists began moving there. It's popularity soon soared. It then became a playground for the Texas elite. High desert ranch land became extremely valuable. Massive retreat homes have replaced the modest ranch houses. A private air strip was built and there are always private jets on the runway. It's bizarre.

Marfa used to literally have dirt cheap homes. Families that have lived there since the town was founded are moving because they can no longer afford to live there.

At night, you can see the Marfa lights just outside of town. The Marfa lights are red, white, yellow and sometimes orange lights that appear on the horizon and then disappear. No one is sure what they are but we've seen them. They're real.

The epic movie *Giant* starring James Dean, Rock Hudson and Elizabeth Taylor was filmed during the summer of 1955 in Marfa. The stars all stayed at the historic and charming El Paisano Hotel. It was built in 1930 by hotel magnate Charles Bassett for cattle ranchers travelling through the vast expanse of West Texas and those with lung ailments seeking the benefits of the dry desert air.

Terlingua is closer to Big Bend. It's home to the Original Terlingua International Chili Cook-Off. This is a huge event. Other than the chili cook-off and the accompanying events, Terlingua is a sleepy little town. This is where you will find the desert rats. People who live here want to be out in the middle of nowhere and as far away from everything as possible. It's a cool little town that hasn't changed at all.

There's a small cemetery there with headstones dating back before Texas was even a state. The most popular place or really the only place to go in town is a small bar/restaurant/concert hall called the Starlight Theatre. On weekends, musicians regularly come to town and play there. Jerry Jeff Walker is a frequent performer.

Eleven miles away, Lajitas sits on a bluff overlooking the Rio Grande directly across from Mexico. It has a nine-hole golf course and a driving range from which you can hit golf balls across the Rio Grande into Mexico. It also has a duly elected beer drinking donkey named Billy the Kid as mayor. He beat the incumbent golden retriever. I told you, people get crazier the closer they live to Mexico.

On one of our road trips, we met some French tourists in Lajitas. They were very disappointed because Billy was not interested in drinking beer the morning they visited him. He had a few too many the night before and wasn't feeling well.

One of the locals suggested they pour some coffee into a beer bottle. They did just that and sure enough Billy took the bottle between his teeth, tossed his head back and chugged the coffee. After a light lunch, Billy had his first beer of the day much to the delight of the Frenchmen. Billy may have had a drinking problem.

Big Bend was weird and fun but if we had at least a week off from school we were headed to Mexico. Robby loved to travel. This is strange for someone so cheap since traveling is an expensive hobby but he only travelled on a shoestring budget. Mexico was perfect for him. It was a cheap and dangerous foreign country. I'm glad I went on all of those trips with him though.

We went all over Mexico. I'm not talking about partying in Cancun on spring break either. On our first trip, we drove from Lubbock to San Diego then to Cabo San Lucas and back. That was the spring break trip of our senior year at Lubbock High. I still can't believe my parents let me go with him.

When I say we traveled cheap, I mean we didn't stay at hotels. We didn't stay at motels either. Sometimes, we didn't stay at campgrounds. Most of the time, we would pull off the road and find a flat spot to throw down a sleeping bag or just sleep in the car. In either case, this is very dangerous and ill-advised, especially in Mexico.

We would always take his car. I never offered and he knew I would never drive my truck across the border. My parents would kill me. He drove a Pontiac Turismo which was perfect because turismo is Spanish for tourism. Sometimes, another friend would go with us but they couldn't handle it. Robby was intense and wanted to travel as far as he could go, do everything there was to do along the way and get there as fast as possible. There wasn't much downtime.

He loved to haggle with Mexican merchants and would low-ball them every time. They would get so mad at him. I would walk away when he did this because it was so embarrassing. We were in a third world country and Robby wouldn't agree to pay two dollars for a handmade chess set. He could give a rat's ass about playing chess!

We saw and did so much. We swam with sea lions around the tip of Baja. We drove to the bottom of Barranas del Cobre (Copper Canyon) which is larger than the Grand Canyon. We hiked to the bottom of Basaseachic Falls, the second highest waterfall in Mexico. We found museums in central Mexico with art by Pablo Picasso. We visited ancient ruins in Chiapas and were chased out of town by tool wielding Zapatistas revolting against the Mexican government. We were detained by the Mexican Army after we escaped from the rebels. A soldier ordered Robby to pull the car over. Robby pulled over and parked in front of a tank. There was a machine gun mounted on the tank and the gunner had the machine gun pointed directly at me.

"Why did you park in front of the tank? You could have pulled up next to the tank instead of parking in front of it. He's got that machine gun pointed right at me. He could sneeze and accidentally pull the trigger! You dick! You did that on purpose."

When the soldier realized we were there on vacation, he looked very confused. He just shook his head and sent us on our way.

Robby also thought it was funny to pick up hitchhikers in Mexico, something else that is ill-advised in the states and especially in Mexico. He finally picked up a hitchhiker that even frightened him. That was the end of that practice. Thank God.

Bribing is a way of life for people in Mexico. We got used to it. One time, I was taken to jail for making a U-turn. Forty dollars got me out. It was ridiculous.

We went scuba diving all along the Mexican coast. We even went diving in one of the cenotes (underwater caves) of the Yucatan peninsula. I thought skydiving was the craziest thing Robby ever talked me into until he got me to dive in a cenote. That makes your butt pucker. If you run out of air, you can't dart to the surface. You drown. Your light goes out and you can't find the way out of the cave, you run out of air and you drown. There's no room for error doing that. I was foolish enough to let Robby talk me into doing it a second time!

Our last trip before we graduated was to Big Bend. We took a bottle of Dom Perignon with us just like in the movie *Fandago*. You need to watch it if you haven't seen it. It was the end of an era.

I met Tamra during my last year of pharmacy school. She was a transplant from Asheville, North Carolina. Robby didn't like her. Of course he didn't, she wasn't foreign. I adored her, though. She was outgoing, charming and had a zest for life. She knew everybody and everybody thought the world of her. I was hooked.

Tamra was an education major. She wanted to be a school teacher. My mating instinct took over. I wanted a woman who could light my fire and be a mother. I thought she was perfect.

Robby thought the relationship was moving too fast. He told me she had a reputation as a girl who'd been around. He suggested Tamra and I get to know each other better before getting too serious. I ignored his advice and asked her to marry me.

After a lustrum in school, I graduated, married Tamra and we moved to Lubbock. I got a job with a nuclear pharmacy which isn't as exciting as it sounds. A nuclear pharmacy compounds nuclear medicine that is used for diagnostic studies. I basically made the donuts and then they were delivered to the hospitals. Tamra had a difficult time finding a job. The teaching market was saturated. She ended up getting a job teaching senior level English in a small town just outside of Lubbock called Richardstown.

At first, she hated living in Lubbock. It was an adjustment for her. Lubbock is nothing like Austin or Asheville. Eventually, she settled into her new job and life in Lubbock. I still had many friends in Lubbock and meeting their wives and girlfriends made her happy. She had a pre-made social life. Ted still lived there. He didn't like Tamra. That may have been the only thing he and Robby had in common.

Tamra and I bought a house and we started talking about having children. We also talked about her spending habits. She spent money as fast as I could earn it. She showed up with a new convertible one day.

"Where's your car?"

"This is my car."

"It is, huh? Where's your OTHER car?"

"I traded it in."

"You did what?"

She decided she wanted a convertible. She said she'd always wanted one and flat dry Lubbock, Texas was the perfect place for it. I was pissed. I wasn't excited about having a new car payment. Our vehicles were paid off and it made no sense to get a new convertible if we were about to start a family. It was an awesome car though, I hate to admit. It was a Chrysler Sebring Limited Edition convertible. I acquiesced. I'd never had a convertible either and I had to admit it was fun. I guess it did have a back seat big enough for a baby seat.

It didn't raise a red flag. She said she had lots of papers to grade and it was just easier to do it after school and then come home. I didn't suspect a thing.

It was a Friday night. We were at Richardstown's homecoming football game. We were sitting in the stands and Tamra was introducing me to her colleagues. At half-time, she told me she wanted to go say hi to her students. I visited with her fellow teachers for a while. Tamra hadn't returned so I went to get a Coke and look for her. I got a Coke but didn't find her. I looked back up into the stands to see if she had returned to our seats. I didn't see her so I walked towards the women's restroom thinking she might be in there. I saw one of the teachers she just introduced me to leaving the restroom.

"Is Tamra in there?"

She was a bit startled when I asked her.

"Oh, you're Tamra's husband. No. No, she's not in there."

"OK. Thanks."

I started to head back to our seats when I saw a group of students behind the stands. They were all looking at something underneath the bleachers. One of them saw me walking their way. He alerted the others and they all scattered. It was very odd. I walked to where they were standing and looked around the corner.

I dropped the Coke.

I turned around and walked to the convertible. I unlocked it, dropped the top and drove back to Lubbock. I parked the car in front of our house. I went inside and I gathered all of her things. I piled them into the convertible. The couch she insisted on buying was hard to get on there but I did it. Her clothes were falling over the sides of the car onto the street. Her school papers were being blown down the street by the West Texas wind. I got everything that belonged to her out of the house. I took the garage door opener from her car and opened the trunk. She left her purse in it. I took her credit card, checkbook and house keys from her purse. I slammed the trunk. I went into the house and packed a bag. I locked all the doors, including the chain locks she insisted I put on for safety. I went out the garage and used her opener to close it as I got into my truck and left.

I dropped the Coke because I saw my wife having sex with one of her students under the bleachers. That's what the other students were watching. I later found out his name was Manuel Pequeno. Manuel Pequeno? Are you kidding me? Pequeno means small in Spanish!

I left Richardstown in a zombie-like state. I was driving home when Tamra called me on my cell phone. I threw it out of the car, along with my wedding ring.

My head was spinning and I had no idea where to go. There was a Tech game the next day and one of the rare conventions in town so there were no hotel rooms available. I went to Ted's house. He was home and let me in.

"Mind if I crash here?"

"Sure man. What's wrong?"

"Tamra's having an affair with one of her students."

"Ouch. That's gotta' hurt. Sorry man."

Ted was never one to mince words.

A sex tape surfaced on the internet the following week. Three months later we were officially divorced and she was on her way back to North Carolina.

Ted and Robby were right about her.

Sand Bottom

I almost missed my flight. I was smoking and getting drunk in the airport bar and lost track of time. As I sat down another empty mug, I glanced at my watch. Shit! My flight was leaving in 23 minutes! I threw down a fifty dollar bill and ran to the terminal. I barely made it to the gate in time. I boarded the plane, found my seat and passed out. I woke up in Honolulu.

The weather couldn't have been nicer but Honolulu is like Dallas on the beach. There are a lot of tall buildings and too many people. I got a bed at the local youth hostel and spent a few days on Oahu.

My first day there I met a group of European travelers. I tagged along with them to happy hour at Duke's Beach Bar. I proceeded to get shit-faced and made a complete ass out of myself hitting on a beautiful Danish woman in the group. I passed out at the bar but the Europeans took pity on me and drug me back to the hostel.

The next morning, after apologizing to everyone for my behavior, I went to Waikiki and gave boogie boarding a try. I wiped out and slammed into some coral. I've got a nice scar from that experience. While on Oahu, I also went to Chinatown and Pearl Harbor. There's not much to see at Pearl Harbor but there's a lot to remember.

On my last day there, I caught a ride to the North Shore with some surfers. We all piled in a van and got stoned on the drive there. When we got there, they surfed and I sat on the beach drinking the best pineapple juice I ever tasted. On the way back, we stopped at the house used in the TV series *Magnum P.I.* I barely remember because we passed another joint around on the drive back from the North Shore and I was baked by the time we got there. The following day I flew to Maui.

I rented a car and drove the "Road to Hana". This is a stretch of highway that runs along the east coast of the island. The road is just turn after turn. There are over 600 curves along the highway. You can't go very fast but you don't want to. At almost every turn, there is a waterfall and natural pools. Most of the road is high above the beach giving you a great visual vantage point. There are 59 bridges. The entire time you are surrounded by tropical rainforest. It's beautiful.

I found a small pool with only enough room on the side of the road for one car to park. I didn't have time to take a shower that morning and I was going to camp that night. I decided to take a bath while I had the chance. I was already wearing my swimsuit so I grabbed my soap and slid into the small natural pool.

I looked around to make sure I was alone. I took off my swimsuit and started lathering up. No one was around but it still felt awkward. I wondered if there were any animals that lived in these pools. Were there any turtles?…fish? Fish! I quickly jumped out of the pool and pulled my swimsuit on. What if there is a Candiru in there? The Candiru, so I have heard, is a small thin slippery fish that is attracted to urea in urine. Supposedly, it will enter a human urethra and once inside will anchor itself with spines. The only way to remove it is surgically. It may be just a myth but I wasn't taking any chances. Forget it! I'll just stink.

I continued driving along the Hana Highway laughing at myself. There were a number of rich and famous people who owned homes along the highway. George Harrison and Charles Lindbergh both owned houses on Maui just off the Hana Highway. Lindbergh was even buried in a small cemetery along the highway. He spent his last years here trying to stay out of the public eye.

I pulled into Hana late in the afternoon. It was a very sleepy, small town. I found a spot outside of town along the beach where I could set up my tent. I was tired and fell asleep before the sun went down. The next morning, I made the reverse drive along the highway back to the central part of the island and then drove up to Haleakala National Park.

The dormant Haleakala volcano, the "House of the Sun", is the main attraction. At the summit of Haleakala is a massive crater 7 miles across. I hiked into the crater hoping to find a silversword. This is the only place in the world where the silversword grows. I only had to hike about a mile before I found one. It's a beautiful plant. Silversword is a perfect name for it. It reminded me of a West Texas cactus.

I hiked around the crater until sunset and then drove to the campsite at the base of the volcano to set up my tent. I was going to get up early and drive to the top of the volcano to watch the sunrise from the top of Haleakala. I met a couple of guys from Austria at the campsite. They wanted to see the sunrise from Haleakala and then hike down the volcano. They asked and I agreed to give them a lift.

It got cold that night. I didn't think about the temperature change at that high elevation. Hawaii is supposed to be shirt and short weather. I couldn't get warm so I got in the rental car. Luckily, it had a heater. I started the car and ran the heater for a while until I finally got warm. I put on three shirts, my only pair of jeans and my raincoat. That was the extent of my cold weather gear.

About an hour before sunrise, the Austrians stumbled out of their tent and we started the drive up the volcano. I followed the line of winding headlights up to the top of the crater. There were about forty people there to see the sunrise. Most were not prepared for the cold weather and stayed in their cars until the last minute. The sunrise was worth it though. It was beautiful. The House of the Sun did not disappoint.

The Big Island was my favorite though. I flew there the next day. I got to see lava up close, too close. I drove the highway from Kailua-Kona to the lava flow spewing from the Kilauea volcano and emptying into the Pacific Ocean. The highway ended into what looked like miles of black billowy cake frosting.

I got out of my rental car and put some water, snacks and a camera in my backpack. There were a lot of tourists milling about and looking at the tall cloud of steam off in the distance. That was where the lava was pouring into the ocean and that is where I was headed. There was a large warning sign listing all types of dangers and precautions but I didn't care. I walked right past it.

It was late in the afternoon when I started my way to the lava. I saw lots of different types of lava rocks along the way. Some were smooth, some were coarse and some were sharp. I noticed some of the ground sounded hollow. About halfway to the flow, I saw small holes in the ground. I found a hole big enough to stick my head in. I looked in and could see light shining through other smaller random holes. It was a lava tube. I couldn't tell how long it stretched. It looked to be about 10 feet deep. I stood up and realized I was standing on top of a lava tube with a very thin exterior. Great, now I'm going to fall through the ground and be incinerated by a river of lava.

I quickly moved away from the holes and did my best to stay off anything that sounded hollow. Then the smell of sulfur hit me. I was getting close. Only a few people hiked all the way out there to see where the lava and the ocean met. They were cautiously watching the lava flow a safe distance from the edge of the cliff. Not me. I walked right past them to the edge of the cliff. It was one of the coolest things I had ever seen. Molten rock was pouring out the side of the cliff. It was like watching a giant water faucet run. As the lava hit the salt water below, it hissed and cracked as it cooled. It was amazing. It's not every day you get to see earth being made.

"Pretty cool, huh?"

I turned to my left. There was a guy standing there who appeared to be about my age.

"Yeah, real cool."

"You wanna' get closer?"

"Sure."

We made our way down to the lava faucet. The smell of sulfur got worse and I could see the glow of lava between the cracks of the fresh ground we were hiking on. It was scorching hot. We climbed about halfway down the cliff to get as close as we could, which was way too close. I even went a little closer to take some pictures. My legs were so hot. It felt like I was straddling a campfire. I lifted my hiking boot and saw the bottom of it was melting. He noticed it too.

"I think it's time to go."

"Yeah."

We were the last tourists to leave. It was getting dark as we headed back. Clouds rolled in and it began to lightning and thunder. I looked back towards Kilauea. It was now dark enough that I could clearly see the glowing lava from Kilauea flowing towards, around and underneath us. This was crazy. What the hell was I doing walking around in an active lava flow?

As the sun went down, it became very difficult to see. There was no light from the moon due to the cloud cover and the lava rock was black. Luckily, my new acquaintance had a flashlight. As I followed him, it began to rain which made the lava rock very slick. Unfortunately, his flashlight beam began to fade. Soon, we could barely see where we were going as the light grew dimmer and dimmer. We decided to keep going instead of spending the night out there in the rain. I slipped on the wet rock and fell on my ass. He turned to see what happened and slipped as well. He let out a scream.

"What's wrong?"

He didn't answer.

He lay unconscious. I stumbled over to him and knelt down beside him. He was coming to. I placed my hand under his head to support it. The back of his head was warm and wet.

"Give me your flashlight."

It was barely working. I aimed the ever-weakening flashlight at my hand. It was covered in blood.

Oh, Shit!

I shined the light on his face. It was covered as well. I wiped the blood off his face and found the point of origin. His forehead was sliced open. I could see bone.

He had hit his head on a sliver of lava that had cooled to a razor sharp edge. As I was taking off my shirt, he slowly lifted his hand to his forehead and felt the cut and blood rushing from it. I placed the shirt on his forehead and applied pressure.

"All right, you've got to keep pressure on it to control the bleeding. I'm going to hike back to my car and get a flashlight. Then, I'm coming back to get you."

"You think you can make it back in the dark by yourself?"

"Are you kidding me? I used to walk around in pitch-black caves. This is nothin'."

"Here, take my keys. I've got a couple of dive lights in my car. Use those."

"You trust me not to steal your car?"

He laughed.

"What's your name?"

"Rick Rousser."

He held out his hand. I shook it.

"David Lemmons."

"Nice to meet you."

"Likewise."

"Be right back, Dave."

I took off. I wasn't as confident as I put on but I knew he needed medical attention. My adrenaline was pumping.

I felt my way along the lava flow with my boot, falling onto it and into large cracks as I made my way. I couldn't see where the ocean met the beach but I could tell how close I was by the sound of the waves crashing. I tried to pay attention to the sound so I knew I was going parallel with the beach and was headed on a straight course. I took a couple of hard falls and got some nasty cuts on my legs. I've got a few scars from those falls.

I had to be getting close. The first thing I could see was the back of the warning sign I disregarded earlier. As I passed it, I turned to look at the sign. I could barely make out the writing. I stepped close enough to look at the list of precautions on the sign. One of them was "Take a flashlight." It should have also mentioned to take extra batteries. I could see where the black icing ended and the road began. I was so relieved to finally make it to the highway and the only two cars parked at the end of it. It took me almost an hour to make it back. I ran to his red Camaro and opened the back. I rummaged hurriedly through his dive bag and found the lights. I slammed the back shut, turned around and raced back.

It was a lot faster going with light to see by. I kept listening to the waves crash to make sure I was going in a straight line again. I almost hiked past him. He called out to me. I was only about fifty feet away from him. Lucky. It took me less than thirty minutes to get back to him. He was all right and happy to be found. The bleeding had stopped. I handed him a light.

"Follow me."

We trudged along the way I baby-stepped earlier and made it back to the cars. I gave Dave his keys. I turned off the dive light and handed it to him. He turned his off, opened the back of his car and threw them in. He opened his cooler and handed me a beer. I twist the bottle cap off and took a gulp. It tasted awesome. He grabbed one and did the same. He tapped my bottle with his.

"Thanks man."

"Glad to help."

He closed the back and walked over to the driver's side door. Dave opened it and sat in the seat. He looked in the rear view mirror and pulled my shirt away from his forehead to see how bad it was. The gash on his forehead was about two inches long and a quarter inch wide. It started to slowly bleed. He pressed my shirt against his forehead.

"Sorry about the shirt. I'm going to the hospital to get this thing stitched up. Hopefully, I haven't ruined my good looks."

"You sure you're ok to drive?"

"I'm good."

"OK, I'll follow you to make sure you get there all right."

"Thanks again."

"You bet. See you at the hospital."

He took off as I got in my rental car. I started the car and pushed in the cigarette lighter. The radio was playing "Can't You

See" by the Marshall Tucker Band. I turned up the volume and lit a cigarette. I took a deep drag and exhaled slowly. Jesus, what a night! I drove off following the quickly disappearing tail lights.

The ER doc was able to stitch him up.

"Nothing bleeds like a head wound."

When we left the ER the sun was just coming up.

"Wanna' grab some breakfast? I'm buyin."

"Don't you have a medical bill to pay for now?"

"Shut up. Let's go eat. I'm starving."

We survived the volcano.

The next day, I caught a flight to Tahiti.

How to Drown

Tahiti is a blur. My drinking picked up. I guess I was still trying to escape from my short and disastrous marriage. There were always fellow travelers to imbibe with. Where they had rooms to return to, often luxurious ones as found in Tahiti, I slept on the beach. I spent the first couple of weeks island hopping and diving almost every day. Between tank dives and bar tabs my finances were rapidly dwindling. I was very tan and very skinny.

One morning, I was sitting on the front step of a dive shop waiting for it to open. I took off my straw hat and sat it upside down in front of me as I ran my fingers through my dirty blond hair. I was wishing my head would stop pounding from the night before. As I sat with my elbows on my knees and my forehead resting in my hands, I heard coins clinking together.

At first, I thought I was having some absurd dream about Vegas but then I realized what happened as I opened my eyes. There, inside my straw hat, were French Polynesian coins. A strolling tourist mistook me for a bum and dropped them in my hat. I guess it wasn't a mistake. I was virtually homeless.

I had a few personal items, some clothes, dive gear, swimsuits, a sleeping bag and a tent. Oh, and a straw hat to panhandle with. My days became routine and pathetic. I'd wake up with a hangover, drink coffee, take ibuprofen, dive, drink and repeat. I was running out of money though. I was homeless and would soon be penniless. Tahiti is unbelievably beautiful but expensive. I met a few budget travelers such as myself and when the topic of next destination came up they all said the same thing. The cheapest, friendliest and most beautiful place to go was Bali, especially the island of Lombock.

I had less than a hundred dollars left after paying for the flight to Bali. I stood out from the rest of the passengers but I showered that morning at least. I had a makeshift shower anyway. I filled a gallon jug with water from the sink in the local bar and liberated a bar of soap from there as well. I found a suitable tree and hung the jug from a branch. I turned the jug upside down and carefully poked several small holes in the base of it with my dive knife.

Once I had enough holes poked, I let the jug hang from the branch and I stood under my "shower". I scrubbed myself with the stolen soap. It felt awesome. It was the cleanest I had been in weeks. I let my clothes air out the night before. My Tech shirt and some khaki shorts were the least dirty and smelly. They would have to do.

As I stood on the tarmac with the other passengers waiting to board our flight, I could feel their stares. They were clad in soft, clean tropical shirts and ironed shorts. Sun hats, Italian leather sandals, Rolexes, gold bracelets, necklaces and rings adorned them. Gucci and other designer luggage stored their luxurious possessions. I, on the other hand, stood in my aforementioned wardrobe. I had my straw hat on my head and my worn out flip flops on my feet. My luggage was a small backpack full of all of my worldly possessions except for the dive gear, sleeping bag and tent I stuffed in my dive bag. I was well overdue for a shave and haircut. I looked pathetic. I was pathetic.

I was so relieved when we finally got to Bali. I wanted to get away from the well-to-do tourists as fast as possible. Not to men-tion, there were so many delays, it took almost 24 hours to finally get there.

I grabbed my dive bag and hiked straight to the beach. I set up my tent and lay down on my sleeping bag. It was extremely humid. It rained cats and dogs just before we landed. I grew accustomed to the humidity but this was ridiculous. I began to think of how dry it is in West Texas. People say it's a dry heat. Yeah, like an oven. But at that moment, it sounded like heaven compared to this heat and humidity.

I awoke to the sunrise and the sound of waves crashing on the beach. I would have appreciated how incredibly beautiful and amazing it was if I didn't feel so horrible. It was time for some much needed coffee and I was starving. I packed my things and made my way back into Mataram, the city where we landed the night before. I found a street vendor and did my best to tell him I needed the least expensive of his delicacies as my finances were quickly dwindling. He finally understood and offered me some leftover nasi jinggo from the night before.

A nasi jingo is basically a Bali burrito. It's not as good as a bean burrito from Taco Villa but it's pretty tasty. Instead of a tortilla, they use a banana leaf. It's filled with rice or noodles, coconut and fried tempeh or shallots. Throw in some local spices and you've got a nasi jinggo. It's usually eaten as a late-night snack. Evidently, the vendor didn't sell out the previous night. He sold me two for the price of one. He didn't have any coffee for sale but gave me a small cup of his own brew. I thanked him and moved on.

I headed toward Senggigi. This is the most popular tourist town on Lombock. It's spectacular. There are white sand beaches below lush tropical mountains and coconut trees. All the while, the extinct volcano of Gunung Agung watches over this piece of paradise. There are hotels, bars, bamboo huts and a few dive shops. There are Hindu temples in the mountains and "massage parlors" along the beach. The sinners and the saints are separated only by a small amount of altitude.

Many of the bars have bar girls who are the same girls in the massage parlors. Luckily, I was forewarned that many of these girls were actually boys. They are known as lady boys. I'm sure some guys found out the hard way. Pun intended.

I found a spot on the beach on the outskirts of town to camp for the night. It was late in the afternoon when I fell asleep. Around midnight, I woke up and couldn't go back to sleep. I got out of my tent and stretched. I grabbed my water bottle and walked down to the waves crashing on the beach. I lay down on the cool sand and gazed at the stars. It was a cloudless night and the stars shined brightly. It reminded me of looking at the stars when Robby and I were driving through the night on our way to Big Bend on one of our many road trips.

Robby… Ted… Tamra… Since I left Lubbock, I tried not to think about anyone or anything. I tried to ignore the emotional pain from the divorce or drown it with alcohol when I couldn't. I was jealous of my friends who were married and had children. I wanted to be married and have children. I wanted a family. I wanted to be normal, to have a normal life and I failed miserably.

I was very depressed and ashamed of my self-pity. No one knew where I was. My mother must have been worried sick. My paid vacation was over weeks ago so I probably didn't have a job to go back to.

I tried not to think about her but Tamra was the first thing I thought of when I woke up and the last thing I thought about before falling asleep. Most nights, I dreamt of her. I couldn't help it. I just couldn't get her off my mind.

The pain in my heart hadn't lessened since the day I saw her and her teenage lover under the stands. My heart was broken and

I didn't know if it was ever going to heal. If only I could fall asleep and never wake up again. I didn't want to live.

I couldn't hold my emotions back any longer. I cried. I sobbed. I wept. I asked God what I did to deserve this. I buried my face in my hands, curled into the fetal position and cried myself to sleep on the beach.

In the morning, I composed myself. I gathered my things and visited the local dive shops hoping to find a job. I wasn't a divemaster but hoped with my experience I might be able to get some work taking tourists on dive trips. Unfortunately, there was no work to be found. One of the local dive operators mentioned a dive shop on the southern end of the island that might need help. So, I walked and hitchhiked my way to Kuta, a town much smaller than Senggigi on the southern tip of Lombock.

Kuta is surrounded by a series of crescent bays with beautiful white sand beaches and crystal blue water. A coral reef runs just outside the bays parallel to the beaches. Waves are good and attract numerous surfers.

There is only one dive shop in this one horse town. It was late when I arrived and the shop was already closed. It was a very plain looking hut. Above the door there was an old surfboard that was painted white and "Diver Dan's" was painted in red letters on it. There was a tattered and sun bleached dive flag hoisted above it that was slowly waving in the gentle breeze. I camped on the beach as usual and returned the next morning.

This is where we met. Tourists knew him as Diver Dan. It wasn't a very original nickname. He hated being called that but it was good for business. His name was Daniel Coker and those who knew him personally called him "Coke".

He was an old SSI (Scuba Schools International) graduate like me. He was also a Texan. Austin was his hometown. He had a full head of bleach blond hair, perfectly straight white teeth and was very tan. He was physically fit and had almost no body fat. I thought he was in his forties but he was actually in his fifties. When I met Coke, I was broke and looked pitiful. I got chiggers from sleeping on the beach and was covered with small red dots. I itched horribly and was miserable. Coke had some local concoction of lotion used to kill the little bastards and gave me some. It felt like heaven. Each layer I slapped on numbed the pain more and more. All Coke could do was laugh.

"Where are you from?" he asked in his thick Texas drawl.

"West Texas."

"West Texas, huh? How the hell did you get here? You go to Tech?"

"Yes Sir."

"Are you from Texas?"

As if I couldn't tell.

"Yep. Born and raised."

"Rick Rousser."

I extended my hand and he shook it.

"Call me Coke."

"Coke?… Like the drink?"

"Yep. Name's Dan Coker but everybody calls me Coke."

"All right. So, this is your dive shop?"

"Yep. Only one in town…or village, rather."

"Need any help?"

"We all need help from time to time."

"How about you? You need some help?"

I laughed.

"Oh, about all I can get."

I started working for him that same day. He let me sleep on a cot in the back of the shop out of chigger range. He couldn't pay me much but I got decent tips. He even got me certified as a divemaster.

Kuta is idyllic but I soon fell back into my old ways. We'd have a couple of dive trips per day then I'd spend the afternoons and evenings drinking with tourists and surfers. Coke never said anything but I could tell he didn't like my carousing. One night, I got really messed up with some surfers. We were drinking tequila and they had the best weed I'd ever smoked. I was already hammered when they pulled out a joint and started passing it around. I took a couple of hits and that's the last thing I remember.

I was halfway in the water from my waist down when I woke up on the beach. I got up on my hands and knees and crawled out of the water. I collapsed on the sand. I laid there for a moment and then rolled over onto my back. I covered my face with my hands to block out the sun as I tried to come to my senses. Where was I? What the hell happened last night? Oh, Shit! I missed the morning dive I was supposed to lead. Coke's going to kill me.

"Have a good night?"

I tilted my head back and saw Coke sitting about 10 feet behind me drinking a cup of coffee. A wave of guilt and shame crashed over me.

"I'm sorry Coke. I had way too much to drink last night. I'm so sorry."

"A man who drinks as much as you do must be trying to forget something."

"Please don't fire me."

"Must be a woman. I bet it's because of a woman."

I moaned as I collapsed back onto the beach.

"So… is it a woman?

"Yes, it's a woman."

"I knew it!"

"Are you going to fire me?"

"No, I'm not going to fire you."

"What happened?"

"I don't remember. I got really messed up."

"No, not that! I know that. The woman. She cheat on you?"

"Ugh, yes."

"I knew it!"

"I'm glad you find it so amusing."

"Well, I've been wondering what it was that got you to abusing yourself so badly. I figured it had to be a woman. You can't run away from it Rick."

"I know."

"Drinking the way you do is just slow suicide. I hate to see you throw your life away. I'm kinda fond of you."

"Ugh."

He walked over to me and stood beside me extending his hand to help me up. I took it and he jerked me to my feet. I swayed there for a moment before he slapped me on the back and we headed for the dive shop. We got there and he handed me a beer as I sat down on a stool at the counter. That took me by surprise. I took a couple of big gulps.

"Thanks. I needed that."

"I know you did."

"Oh man, I feel horrible."

"You look it too."

"You've got to stop doing this to yourself."

"Yeah, I know."

He slammed his fist on the counter.

"Then stop it! You almost drown!"

I was startled. I had never seen Coke mad before.

"Were you married?"

"Yes."

"You get a divorce?"

"Yes."

"Where did you live?"

"Lubbock."

"What did you do there?"

"I was a pharmacist."

"So, you gave up and ran away."

"No."

"Yes, you did."

"Ugh."

"Well, you've run away from your problem. Now what?"

"I don't know."

I took another drink.

"So, your woman done you wrong and you decided to just take off? Any final destination in mind?"

"No."

"Are you going to work for me for the rest or your life?"

"I don't know where I'm going or what I'm going to do."

"Well, I do. You're going to pull yourself together, go home and get your life back."

"What if I don't want to go? It's a moot point anyway. I can't afford to fly home."

"I'll buy you a plane ticket."

"I can't let you do that."

"You don't have a choice."

"I don't want to leave. I love it here. Why are YOU here? What did YOU run away from!?"

"I killed my wife and daughter."

His words sent chills running up and down my spine.

I sat frozen in stunned silence.

"I was drunk and driving them home."

He looked away. He stared out at the beach.

"I'm sorry."

"Me, too."

"What did you before you came here, Coke?"

I was trying to think of anything to change the subject. He poured himself some more coffee.

"I was a petroleum engineer and an Ironman."

"You worked with oil and iron?"

"No, I worked as a petroleum engineer and was a Ironman triathlete."

"You mean like the triathlon in Hawaii? The one where that lady crawled across the finish line?"

"Yep, that's the world championship."

"How long is the race?"

"2.4 mile swim, 112 on the bike and then you run a marathon."

"And then you run a marathon?!"

"I can't imagine. I could never do that."

"Yes, you could."

"I doubt it."

"Don't ever doubt yourself. I don't."

"Whatever possessed you to do that?"

"I was a swimmer at UT. One of my friends on the team was into doing triathlons and told me to try it out. So, I did. It was a sprint triathlon. I did well on the swim of course but I was using an old ten-speed bicycle that slowed me down on the bike portion. I had a decent run and managed to finish in ninth place. I signed up for another triathlon the very next day. I was hooked.

I got a good bike and started riding it wherever I went. I also worked on improving my running. I quickly realized I had terrible form and was a heel striker. I was a fast runner but running was never my thing. I kept competing in triathlons. Some I did really well in and won a few. Some I did very poorly in.

It takes time to learn how to compete in a triathlon. You learn how to shave time off your swim, bike and run. Pacing yourself is crucial. Hydration and nutrition are important. Quick transitions, focus and determination during the race can make all the difference. I learned the hard way just because you win the swim doesn't mean you win the race. It's who wins the run that matters."

I never heard him talk so much or so passionately about anything else besides diving. I had no idea he ever even did a triathlon. Coke and I got along very well and became good friends but we didn't talk much about our pasts.

"I turned pro and qualified for Kona. Man, I was so nervous but excited. The days leading up to it are brutal. Those were the longest days of my life. The energy of the people in the pre-dawn morning of the race is palpable! There are lights and people everywhere. Announcers are on loud speakers giving last minute instructions. There is a beehive of activity. People are warming up, checking their gear in transition and trying to act calm. You hear the sound of tires being aired up all around you. The mood is emotionally charged. There are cameras, TV helicopters, spectators and a beautiful sunrise over Mt. Hualaai. Rick, I've never felt that level of excitement and raw nerves as the few seconds before they fired the cannon to start the race!

It was a frenzy of arms and legs flailing in Kailua Bay. Right off the bat, I screwed up. I took the lead in the swim. I led the first third of the swim but realized I pushed too hard. My breathing was labored and my arms felt heavy. I let the excitement of the race get the best of me. Before the turn at the halfway point, four guys passed me. Another four passed me before the swim was over. I was so glad to get out of the water.

I made a mad dash to my bike as I pulled my cap and goggles off. I threw on my helmet and sunglasses, ripped my bike off the rack and sprinted to the bike mount. Man, I jumped on my bike like I was a cowboy jumping in the saddle. I started pedaling and got my speed up then strapped my feet in my shoes. I put the hammer down as I rode along the Queen Ka'ahumanu Highway from Kailua-Kona to the turnaround in Hawi.

The heat coming off the surrounding black lava rock bordering the road was intense. The wind wasn't that bad getting there but on the way back it was brutal. The wind coming off the ocean picked up and would knock me into the middle of the road. I passed a couple of guys on the first half of the bike but now I was being passed.

I was exhausted when I got back to Kailua-Kona. I was dizzy and my ass hurt so badly when I got back to transition. The transition to the run was not a smooth one. I made my way through town and barely noticed the spectators packed along the run course. I ran along Ali'i Drive up to Palani Road and back onto the Queen Ka'ahumanu Highway.

I was hurting. It was hot and humid and I was spent. I didn't even make it halfway through the run before I had to stop running and start walking. I never had to walk before. I walked for about half a mile before I started running again. After two miles, I had to walk again. I was exhausted but still had enough energy to be thoroughly disgusted with myself. I kept telling myself, "I'm better than this." I wasn't that day though. It took me over four hours to finish the run."

"Wow. Even if you didn't win, that's still amazing you could do all that."

"I was pretty dejected though. Stephanie, my wife, and Lauren, our daughter, greeted me at the finish line and hugged me like I won the race. They kept telling me how proud they were of me. I didn't feel very proud. When we got home, I had time to reflect and realized how fortunate I was just to be able to compete at that level. In the triathlon world, qualifying for Kona is like making it to the Superbowl. I was very frustrated but determined to do better when I made it back to Kona.

I did make it back to Kona and won on my third attempt. It was unbelievable. It still is. Stephanie and Lauren greeted me at the finish line as they always had. They hugged me and I realized something. Their hugs were exactly the same as they gave me after every race. They didn't squeeze me or hold me any differently than if I just lost. They were sincerely proud of me and been equally proud of me after every race I was in. It didn't matter to them if I was a triathlete, an Ironman, the World Champion or a petroleum engineer. They were proud of me and loved me."

"That's nice."

"Of course, I'm very glad to have won but realizing how lucky I was to have my wife and daughter in my life was even better. I appreciate what I have learned about people and myself from doing triathlons. It's hard to explain but you develop a longing to keep doing them even as difficult as they are, to keep getting better and to encourage others. But the best is to cross the finish line with your family waiting to greet you and tell you how proud they are of you."

His demeanor suddenly changed.

"After they died in the car wreck, I only did one more triathlon. I sprinted across the finish line as I always had. My name was announced and I stopped to catch my breath. There was no one at the finish line to hug me and tell me how proud they were of me. I rushed away from the finish line and darted down an alley. I had to stop because I couldn't see.

Tears were streaming down my face. I had lost the most important part of the triathlon, the most important people in my life. They weren't there. I was devastated and guilt stricken after the wreck. I hadn't cried yet. I didn't allow myself to cry because it was my fault they were dead. I didn't even go to their funeral because I was so ashamed of myself.

I only visited their gravesites after everyone was gone. I told them how sorry I was and how much I loved them. I begged them to forgive me and left flowers at their headstones. Now, I couldn't stop crying. I collapsed behind a dumpster and wept for them."

"I'm sorry Coke. You're not a bad person. You've been a good friend to me. You just made a bad decision."

"A horrible one, the worst I will ever make. I was on top of the world when I became the world champion. I partied like I was a rock star.

I was ejected from the car. They were trapped in the wreckage. The car caught fire and they burned to death. The only reason I didn't go to prison was because by the time they gave me a breathalyzer test and made me do all of the field sobriety tests my blood alcohol level had dropped to a legal level. I know I was drunk though. I deserve whatever misfortune befalls me."

He left and started slowly walking to the beach. I didn't see him again until the next day. There was an awkward silence between us throughout the day. After our last dive, he finally spoke to me.

"I shouldn't have told you all of that yesterday."

He looked me straight in the eye.

"I want you to go home."

"Go home? I don't want to go home. I love it here."

"Just, go at least. If you want to come back, there will always be a place for you here. A failed marriage is not a tragedy. It sucks but it's not a tragedy. Unfortunately, it's all too common these days. At least half of marriages end in divorce. I'm sure it's a very painful experience but you're strong enough to recover from it. I'll buy you a ticket. All you have to do is get on the plane."

"Why do you want me to go home so bad?"

"I want you to get closure. You can't get that here. You tried to run away from your problem and you failed. The problem is still within you. Go home. Face reality. Get your head on straight. Please Rick. If not for yourself, do it for me."

I knew he was right and I'd learned there was no arguing with Dan Coker.

"All right, I'll go. But I'm coming back!"

"Fine. I want you to do me a favor though."

"Sure. What's that?"

"Check out the half Ironman at Buffalo Springs Lake."

"There's an Ironman in Lubbock?"

"Half Ironman. It's a great race. Very tough. Good preparation for Kona, especially with the wind and heat. That's where I got my first Kona slot."

"Ok. I'll check it out."

I was on a plane three weeks later.

Lombock to Lubbock

I had plenty of time to think on my long journey home. I wasn't thinking about Tamra anymore. I was thinking about my future. I'd been reading a book about the Gestapo to pass the time on the numerous flights it took to get home. It got me thinking about an elective class I took at Tech, History of Nazi Germany. It was a great class. I really enjoyed it and even toyed with the idea of changing my major to history. There's not a great demand for historians so I decided to stick with pharmacy.

Why not do it now? I was single and could do whatever I wanted. I could work part-time and study history in graduate school.

Flying into Lubbock, I was happy. I was surprised and it was strange. As I looked out the window, I was glad to see all of the flat farmland dotted with playa lakes. It felt good to be home. We flew into the Lubbock International Airport, which is a misnomer. It's basically a hub to DFW.

My grandfather was picking me up from the airport. I always wanted to ask my grandfather about his experience during the war but was afraid to do so. Now, I was going to ask him. My trip into depravity and self-pity had some positive results at least. I wasn't afraid to do anything. This was not because I had nothing to lose but rather because I felt strong as an individual. I had done a lot, seen a lot and learned a lot about the world as well as myself. I met some good people. I realized people can be the best and the worst thing in your life. You just have to surround yourself with the best. I may not have acted very mature but I matured at least.

The landing was a little rough due to a strong cross wind. This was not unusual at the Lubbock airport. My grandfather was waiting for me at the luggage carousel.

"Are you done feeling sorry for yourself?"

"Yes, Grossvater."

"Good."

We waited in awkward silence for the luggage to arrive. My grandfather only spoke when he felt like it. He was never one to chit-chat. My bag finally appeared.

"Is that all of your luggage?"

"Yes, Grossvater."

"Let's go."

He was impatient as always. I threw my bag into the back of his black 1969 Chevrolet El Camino SS.

"Don't scratch my truck dummkopf!"

It cracked me up when he called his El Camino a truck. His car had an eight track player but I doubt it worked or that he even owned an eight track. At least the air conditioner still worked. It was at least 100 degrees outside.

He was my only relative in Lubbock now. My brother moved to San Francisco and started some .com companies. I'm sure he's a multi-millionaire by now. My parents socked away enough money to retire in San Diego. I was very happy for them. They were happy to hear I was coming back to Lubbock and were planning to visit me after I got settled in.

"Where do you want to go?"

"Ted's house."

"Am I supposed to know where he lives?

Grumpy old man.

"The corner of 42nd and Tennessee."

"Good, not far from my house."

"He knows you are coming?"

"He knows. I called and asked if I could stay with him."

"You need to find a job."

"That's first on my list."

"Do you have any money?"

"A little."

"I no have extra money for you."

Cheap bastard.

"I may just work part-time and go back to school."

"Education is good but expensive. You study more pharmacy?"

"No, actually I was going to study history."

"History? What good is it to study history? You don't need to know history for pharmacy. You should study more pharmacy."

"I don't know if I want to be a pharmacist anymore."

"What? Why not?"

"I want to be a historian. I'll have to get a PhD and teach at a university but that's all right by me."

"Dummkopf."

He shook his head as we pulled up to Ted's house.

"Is this his house?"

"Yes sir."

"I need to ask you something grandfather."

"What is it? You need money?"

"No grandfather. I'm going to need your help when I go back to school."

"You want me to help you study?"

"No. I want you to tell me about the war."

He stared at me. It reminded me of how Coke looked at me when he told me about his wife and daughter. It also sent chills up and down my spine.

"Nein."

He looked away.

"Grandfather, please. I've never asked you for anything. I need your help. In the short history of mankind, World War II is by far the most significant event to occur. Other than an asteroid wiping out the dinosaurs, nothing else has had such a profound effect on the planet. I want to do my thesis on it. I have all the prerequisites to start my master's. Please Grossvater, I need this. I want to know the history but I also want to know your history. You're my grandfather and I don't have any idea what you did in the war. Please grandfather. Having a first-hand account would be essential for my thesis."

"You don't know what you ask of me. That was a long time ago and nothing good to remember."

"I understand but you're my grandfather and I want to know. I won't write anything bad about you. I promise. I need this. I was devastated after the divorce. I took it harder than I should have. I want to start over. I really want to do this. Maybe it will be good for you to talk about it too."

"I must think on it."

"Thank you! Thank you, grandfather!"

I almost jumped out of the car as I opened the door. I wanted to skip as I headed for Ted's front door. My grandfather honked the horn and I ran back hoping he was going to say yes. I opened the passenger door.

"Yes Sir?"

"You forgot your bag."

"Oh, right. Thank you Grandfather."

I closed the door and grabbed my bag out of the back of his "truck". I headed to the house. My truck was parked on the far side of Ted's driveway, right where I left it before I fled to Hawaii.

He wasn't home but he left a key in the mailbox. As I entered the house, it was evident Ted was doing a lot of hunting and fishing as the walls were lined with taxidermied animals. The first bedroom was filled with junk but the second was empty. It wasn't filthy but his house wasn't clean either, not that I'm a clean freak. I'd definitely been living in more squalid conditions.

I threw my bag in my new room and headed to the kitchen. I opened the fridge, grabbed a beer and headed to the back patio. I sat down in an old patio chair and cracked open the beer. I took a couple of big gulps. It was my first beer since the morning Coke found me on the beach. I pulled a pack of cigarettes and a lighter out of my pocket. I lit a cigarette and blew a smoke ring. Ted came bounding through the back door.

"Rick! Man, I'm glad to see you."

He gave me a big bear hug, which surprised me as Ted wasn't the affectionate type at all.

"When did you start smoking again?"

"Hawaii."

"You gotta' quit that."

"Yeah, I know."

"So, where you been? How you been? You're a tan, skinny little bastard, aren't ya!"

"I've been to Hawaii, Tahiti and Bali. Diving and drinking mainly."

"Well you can do one of the two here. Been anywhere that doesn't end in an "i"? I'm gonna grab a beer."

He slapped me on the back. It hurt. I forgot how strong he was.

We stayed up drinking past midnight. I told him about my adventures. He filled me in on his hunting trips. We reminisced and laughed about old times. We ran out of beer and that was a good thing. We didn't need any more.

I woke up with a horrible headache. I rolled off the couch and stumbled down the hall to Ted's room. He was face down like a reverse snow angel.

"You awake?"

"Unfortunately. How much did we drink last night?"

"Too."

"Ugh."

"I'll go get us some Taco Villa. Where are my truck keys?"

"Top dresser drawer."

He didn't move through the whole conversation. Ted was lying on the couch and watching golf when I got back. I hate golf. It's so boring and I suck at it. He sat up and I threw him a burrito.

"I made some coffee."

"Good man."

I went to the kitchen and found one of few clean coffee mugs. I poured myself a cup. I burnt my mouth taking the first sip but I needed it bad. I hadn't tied one on like that since the night before Coke found me on the beach. I found some ibuprofen and took four of them. I joined Ted in the living room and ate my breakfast burrito.

I kicked back in the recliner and fell asleep. Golf was good for one thing - napping. I woke up late in the afternoon and we got calzones from One Guy for dinner. One Guy from Italy is a family-owned and operated pizzeria in Lubbock known for their fantastic calzones. It was good to be home.

I started job hunting the next day. I got a part-time job at Eckerd Pharmacy working evenings and weekends. I didn't care as long as I had a job. There is never a dull moment working at Eckerd. People on Medicaid who drive Cadillacs complain when the have a $1.00 copay. Drug addicts come in to buy syringes and get their "hydros" (hydrocodone) filled. Boxes of allergy decongestants containing pseudoephedrine disappear from the shelves only to reappear on the streets chemically altered into methamphetamine.

Everyone wants to refill their prescriptions without refills on Friday afternoons when all the doctors are on the golf course. Children who only need a good spanking are prescribed Ritalin. "Can I drink with this medication?" is the only question I ever get. Besides hydrocodone, Viagra and Prozac are the two most commonly prescribed medications.

Half the customers use motorized scooters. Some days, it's like watching bumper cars at the South Plains Fair. One of the scooter gang has a very squeaky scooter. You can tell where she's at in the store and which direction she is going by how faint or loud the squeak is. She's also the one who always wears a Chicago Cub's souvenir batting helmet.

There is another customer who is in the store almost every day and only wears a Wolverine t-shirt. I'm not sure if that's the only shirt he wears or if he's got one for every day of the week. My bet is it's the same shirt judging from how dirty it is and how bad he smells. When it's cold he wears a matching Wolverine beanie. He REALLY likes Wolverine.

I prefer working there when it's cold because people wear more clothes. I don't have to see their sickening sandaled feet and the cold lessens their chronic halitosis and foul body odor. There are a disturbing number of morbidly obese women who keep their cash in their bras. I do not perform cashier duties.

All I cared about was getting into graduate school. I was so happy when I was accepted into Tech's Masters program with Dr. Eilam Biterman as my mentor. He was the professor who taught the History of Nazi Germany course I took years ago.

After World War II, Dr. Biterman immigrated to the United States and earned his PhD at Northwestern. Out of his family, he was the only one to survive the war. His family was from a small town outside of Warsaw. They were forced to move and "live" in the Warsaw ghetto during the Nazi occupation. As the ghetto was being liquidated, he managed to escape. His aunts, uncles, cousins, grandparents, parents and siblings did not. They were forced into cattle cars and sent to Auschwitz. Poland's Jewish population was virtually wiped out during the war.

His real life experience and gift of oratory gave his lectures a deeper meaning. I was very fortunate to have him as my mentor.

I was happy. I was doing something I had a passion for and found someone to lead the way. This is also when I met Addison.

I was walking through the Student Union Building on my way to the library and saw a beautiful brunette with blonde hair, tan skin and long legs. Her hair was pulled back in a ponytail and she was wearing a t-shirt, shorts and sandals. She was having a slice of pepperoni pizza and drinking a Coke for lunch. She was reading the Pharmacy College Admission Test Review. Well, there's an "in" I thought to myself. Besides, he who hesitates masturbates. I've got nothing to lose. Screw it. I'm going to talk to her.

"Do you need a reference?"

She looked up at me indignantly.

"Excuse me?"

"Do you need a reference?"

"For what?"

"Pharmacy school."

"No. I'm all right. Thank you."

She continued reading. I wasn't done trying though.

"Mind if I sit down?"

She looked back up at me, leaned back and cocked her head to the side.

"What do you want?"

"I'm a pharmacist."

"Then… why aren't you in a pharmacy?"

"I'm studying history."

"History? Why is a pharmacist studying history?"

"Why not?"

"Well, I'm busy."

She went back to reading her book.

"Ok. Nice to meet you."

She rolled her eyes and shook her head.

Well, it was a pathetic attempt but at least I tried. I decided to skip the library and go run at Tech Terrace Park. I signed up for a sprint triathlon. Coke just raved on and on about how much he enjoyed doing them I figured I would try it out. It would make him happy if he knew I at least tried. That was all the inspiration I needed. I knew he wanted me to do the half Ironman at Buffalo Springs Lake but I wasn't so sure. A sprint triathlon was all I was willing to attempt right now.

I wasn't off to a good start with my training. I could barely swim three laps without running out of breath. I was swimming laps, or trying to anyway, at the YWCA. I had to compete with grumpy old ladies for pool time and they did not like having me on their turf. The old men there aren't afraid to strike up a conversation while standing buck-naked in the locker room.

There was one centurion who was always at the pool. He made a point of talking to me every time I went to swim laps. I never saw him talking to anyone else. It was like I was his confidant. One day, he asked me if I spit in my goggles to clear them. This is an odd question as everyone uses spit to clear their goggles. I told him I did and then he proceeded to tell me he used to but now he licks them. Licks them? Why would you tell someone that? That's creepy. He was an odd duck.

At least on the bike no one could talk to me. I was good on the bike. I wrecked my first car and a bicycle was my only mode of transportation for a long time after that. I even rode my bicycle to Santa Fe and back one summer. A Cannondale racing bike was my high school graduation present. I took my old Cannondale over to the bike shop and got it ready to ride. Bicycle technology had advanced considerably since I used to ride, especially for triathlon bikes. Mine used to be a racecar now it was a jalopy. It was almost twice as heavy as the new tri bikes. I wasn't about to spend thousands of dollars on a tri bike though. They cost too much and I didn't have very much money. The only bad thing about the bike was riding it in Lubbock. I swear people here are the worst drivers on the planet.

When I was running, I wished a car would hit me to put me out of my misery. I couldn't run a mile without feeling like my body was going to fall apart. My knees felt like they had no cartilage. My right foot hurt like I had a bone spur. I didn't know if I could pull this off.

I was sitting on a park bench along the jogging trail at Tech Terrace Park with my shoe off. I was bent over rubbing the bottom of my foot. It was killing me. I needed a break any way. My lungs were burning. I had to quit smoking.

She was walking her dog. I looked up when she stopped and her shadow cast upon me. Her face was silhouetted against the sun. I sat up and used the palm of my hand to block the sun. I squinted and could make out her face. I recognized her. It was the woman I hit on earlier in the day.

"What seems to be the trouble?"

I was surprised to see her and even more surprised that she stopped to talk to me. I didn't really want to talk to her now. I was embarrassed about hitting on her but how else was I supposed to meet women?

"Feels like a bone spur."

"Hhm. You should get better insoles and running shoes."

"Oh, really? You an expert on running apparel?"

"No, but I know the right shoes are important. So is good running form. You've probably got poor running form as well."

I wasn't in the mood for constructive criticism.

"Thanks for the advice."

After my sarcastic appreciation, I put my shoe back on. I was irritated because I knew she was probably right. I decided I wasn't in the mood to chitchat no matter how pretty she was.

"Well, I've got to get back to running poorly in my crappy shoes. So, if you'll excuse me…"

I stood and turned away from her, about to start running poorly in my crappy shoes.

"So… you're a pharmacist trying to be a historian… trying to be a runner."

I stopped.

"Why are you trying so hard to be what you're not?"

I turned around. She was beautiful but also smart and feisty. I could see it in her eyes. I looked down at her dog. She had a beautiful chocolate lab.

"Who's your friend there?"

"This is Bailey."

"Beautiful chocolate lab. Labs are great dogs."

"You an expert on labs?"

"No, but I know the right dog is important."

"All right if I walk with you and Bailey around the park? I think I'm through running for the day."

"I thought you'd never ask."

"What's your name?"

"Addison Haymaker."

"Nice to meet you. I'm Rick Rousser."

We walked around the park telling each other about ourselves. She was from Houston and it sounded like her family had money. She came to Tech because her mother and father went to Tech. They told her she could go to Tech or pay for her own college. She took the offer.

It worked out well. Tech just opened a pharmacy school. Unfortunately, it opened a few years too late for me. I would have saved a lot of money if I could have gone to pharmacy school at Tech but then I would have missed out on having a crazy roommate to do ridiculously dangerous things with.

It turned out she did know what she was talking about. She was a runner in high school. So, maybe I did need different shoes. I already knew my running form sucked.

As we walked around the park talking, my heart was trying to jump out of my chest. I was so attracted to her. I was excited but also terrified. I tried to be cool and play it off but I doubt it worked. I found a Frisbee someone left behind.

"Can Bailey fetch?"

"Of course, she's got good looks and brains just like me."

"At least she doesn't talk as much."

She laughed and took Bailey off her leash. I threw the Frisbee. Bailey sprinted about twenty feet before leaping into the air and catching it.

"Impressive."

"Yes, she is."

Yes she is, I thought. I got her number. I waited three days to call her, that being the normal wait time for a guy to call a girl when I was dating. It was agony. I wanted to call her as soon as I got home from the park that day. We went on our first date less than a week after our afternoon in the park. I moved out of Ted's and into her house a month later.

I should have been more cautious but I couldn't help myself. Hopefully, I chose wisely this time. It wasn't love at first sight, at least not for her.

The First Interview

I was encased in white but could only see black. I was suspended in ice and snow. I could barely breathe. My left hand was in front of my face while my right arm was outstretched. My legs were bent and trapped beneath me. How long was I unconscious? My head was pounding. My ears were ringing. What happened? It didn't matter. I had to get out.

I could move my left hand and I dug towards my right with it. My glove prevented any progress so I pulled it off with my teeth. I clawed away at the ice and snow while twisting my torso. I was able to pull my right arm to my body. I pulled off the right glove with my teeth.

With both hands I clawed upwards. A faint light began to shine through. I could make out the silhouette of my hands. I dug faster. The flesh on my fingertips tore and my fingernails ripped from their beds as I tried to claw my way out. The air became stagnant and my breathing labored. I was running out of air! I panicked.

I punched the snow and ice that was going to suffocate me. I jabbed furiously at it while screaming at the top of my lungs! Finally, my right fist broke through. I retracted my arm and contorted my body to get my mouth as close to the opening as possible. I gasped for air. The bitter cold shot down my throat and seared my lungs. I began a convulsive coughing spell which caused me to dry heave numerous times.

There was nothing to vomit since there was nothing to eat. Food was one of the many things the bitch Russian winter took from us. And now she was determined to take me as well. Hell is supposed to be a raging inferno. Forget that! It's covered in ice and the wind never stops blowing!

I gathered my scarf around my mouth. Once I controlled my breathing, I wrapped the scarf tightly around my face and neck. By this time, my hands were numb, bloodied and useless. The blood on my fingertips dried so quickly it looked as if my fingernails were sloppily painted. Blood red is definitely my color. I gathered my gloves and bit into the bottom of them. I used my teeth to pull them onto my frozen hands. My hands were no longer useful digging tools and it was wise to save them if I could.

I was almost free save for my right leg but I was completely exhausted. I dug my elbows in the snow on each side of me and pushed down on them with all my might. I still couldn't free it. I thrust myself forwards, backwards and side to side. I couldn't get out. I flailed around like a wild man. I lurched myself forward violently twisting my body like a corkscrew. I felt and heard the snow crack. My left leg shook uncontrollably as I put all my weight on it pulling my right leg free. I collapsed.

I sat there having barely dug myself out of my own grave. I stood up and lifted my head out of the small hole to survey my surroundings. The wind struck me in the face like a thousand pins. With the arctic blast and driving snow it was impossible to see anything. I cowered back into the hole. I clutched my frozen hands to my chest as I curled into the fetal position. How could I have any illusions of survival? Why did I even dig my way out?

If the others had been buried as I was, they were surely dead by now. I barely escaped in time. Exhaustion finally overtook me and I fell asleep.

I was very surprised when I awoke, astonished really. How could I still be alive? I hadn't slept long or else I wouldn't be. I was shaking uncontrollably from the cold. It felt as though every muscle in my body was contracting. My teeth were clenched and grinding as I shook. My neck was trying to pull my head inside my body cavity. My balls were already there. My hands throbbed. The sensation in my legs ended mid-calf.

I decided I could continue to freeze to death or I could take what little energy I had left and die trying to live. It was a ridiculous notion to just give up now. I already endured so much it made no sense to quit now. I rubbed my hands together and worked my fingers. It was painful but I could move them. I began to massage my calves and bend my ankles. Soon, I could feel my ankles and move my feet.

I enlarged the opening of my would-be casket and climbed my way out. The wind slapped me in the face again. It took numerous times for me to stand. I still could not feel my toes but I could walk. I walked with the wind at my back. I had no idea which way I was going but I was too weak to walk against it even if that were the way to go. I leaned back and used the force of the wind to keep me upright and moving forward. I thought if I could keep putting one foot in front of the other the arctic blast might push me all the way back to Germany.

I crossed my arms and shoved my hands into my armpits. I clutched myself as tightly as possible. I dug my chin into my chest and raised my shoulders to my ears. I walked, I stumbled, and I fell over and over again. I don't know how many times. I just kept up this pathetic pattern. I didn't expect to live. I just decided not to quit. I was going down swinging.

A sudden gust of wind knocked me down flat on my face. Blood flowed from my nose but in an instant it was frozen. Now I had a red mustache to match my freshly painted nails. It was insult to injury.

The tears from my watering eyes almost froze them shut. I had to use the back of my glove to pull down my cheek and lower eyelid to prevent this. I stood and continued to walk. I fell again but this time I tripped over something. It was the body of a Russian soldier. He was face up. His brown eyes were frozen. His mouth was open and filled with snow. His arms were partially extended to the heavens and his bare hands were grotesquely contorted. The rest of him was covered with snow. Was this soon to be my fate?

I no longer had the strength to stand. All I could do was crawl and I crawled right into it - a Russian tank. I struggled to my feet and attempted to climb upon it. I needed to get inside to take shelter. The sun was starting to set and the temperature was about to drop even more. It felt like I was climbing a mountain. It took several minutes for me to finally reach the turret. I fell head first into the tank and was knocked unconscious.

It was dark outside when I awoke. I had a pounding headache. I rolled over and looked out the turret. Stars shone brightly. I closed the hatch hoping to keep as much heat inside the tank as possible. It wasn't much warmer inside but the tank provided a highly needed reprieve from the wind. I felt around in the dark and found my helmet. I put it on and sat up. My eyes began to adjust to the dark. I could make out the inside of the tank. I was not alone.

He sat across from me. His head was cocked to the left as if studying me inquisitively. Maybe he was admiring my rosy mustache. He didn't blink. He won the staring contest. He won because he was dead. I would rather he were alive. Misery loves company.

I drug myself over to him. He was wearing a ushanka, the traditional Russian winter hat. I quickly traded my helmet for it. His overcoat, valenki boots and gloves were better than mine as well. His army was prepared for the winter. Ours was not.

It was almost impossible to get that coat off his frozen body. I donned my new apparel. I found a satchel. Inside there was a metal cup and a small piece of bread.

I nearly chipped a tooth trying to take a bite. I licked the frozen morsel and breathed upon it until I could ingest a semi-thawed chunk. It tasted of diesel fumes but I didn't care. It was food. I continued this process until the last saliva-laden piece was consumed. I opened the hatch and scooped snow into the cup. I closed the hatch and sat down. I searched inside the satchel again and found a spoon. I stirred the snow and breathed upon it. I held the cup close to my chest. I couldn't get it to melt. It was too cold. I spooned in bites of snow to melt in my mouth for hydration. What I would have given for a hot cup of coffee!

I lay there digesting my feast. Where was I on the battlefield? Had our position been over run? The last thing I remembered were the Russian tanks quickly approaching our position. Shells were exploding all around us. I was outside the tank keeping the fire under the engine from going out. Perhaps a shell exploded nearby knocking me unconscious. Did the force from the explosion bury me in the snow? Had a tank rolled over me? Was it this tank? I laid there in my new apparel contemplating what to do next.

My only hope was to try to find my way to the front and rejoin the Wehrmacht. My original company was decimated. A fortnight ago, I saw my best friend killed by a mortar shell. I had enough of war. But where was the front line now? We almost made it to Moscow. I couldn't believe it! The winter defeated us. I was doubtful the Russian army could be stopped. Their numbers never decreased. They were always able to replenish their troops. Now I looked like another one of their replacements.

I could sound like one too. I learned to speak Russian from my grandmother. She was a German Russian. That is to say she was a German who was born and raised in Russia.

They were called Volksdeutsche, which simply translates to German folk or German people. Her family maintained their German culture but she also learned about the Russian culture and how to speak their language. She and her family moved back to Berlin after the Great War. She would only speak to me in Russian so I had to learn it.

If I was behind enemy lines, perhaps I could blend in with the Red Army. It was possible. Anything was possible. War taught me that. I could make my way back to the Wehrmacht. I might even get to see my family again. My family! I didn't even think of them until now. How could I not have thought of them until now? My wife, Lena, my daughter, Magda and my son, Ulrich were safe 2,000 kilometers away in Germany. They were safe for now at least. They were all the reason I needed to keep going.

I tried to sleep but I was too cold. I couldn't get comfortable and my body ached all over. I wiggled my toes and rubbed my hands together. I could not get warm. Morning finally came and light entered the tank. I studied my deceased comrade. I decided to do it.

I stripped his uniform off and removed mine. Putting on his uniform was like putting on a sheet of ice. It was so cold. I quickly put the ushanka, overcoat and felt boots on. I climbed out of the tank that housed me for the night. I was ready to get moving again to warm myself up. The wind calmed and the snow lessened. I slid down the side of the tank and balanced myself against it. I lifted my scarf above my nose and pulled the ushanka tightly on my head. Again, I walked with the wind at my back. It wasn't blowing as hard now but it still helped hold me up.

Again, I would fall, pick myself up and continue. I walked for hours. I could see my feet shuffling under me but could not feel them. I didn't have the energy to go much farther. Once I could no longer walk, I would have to crawl. Once I could no longer crawl, I would collapse and freeze to death. That's what I had to look forward to.

Before I knew what happened, I was face down in the snow. It felt like someone stabbed me in my backside but it was a bullet. A hot bullet was lodged in my frozen ass.

"Who are you?! Identify yourself!"

Someone was yelling at me in Russian.

"Don't shoot! Don't shoot!"

I replied in Russian, of course.

"Who are you?! Answer me!"

I looked behind me. He was partially hidden behind a tree and still had his rifle pointed at me.

"I'm a soldier with a bullet in his ass! Put down the gun and come help me!"

He cautiously approached me. He didn't shoulder his weapon until he looked me over. He pulled me up but I couldn't put any weight on my leg without a sharp pain in my right buttock and my knee buckling.

"Wait here."

Where the hell was I going to go?

He returned with another soldier. Each of them grabbed a hand and pulled me through the snow. They drug me about 100 meters before lifting me up and helping me into a Dacha, a small Russian hut.

They laid me face down on the dirt floor. It felt like heaven. I know the temperature inside was barely above freezing but it felt like dipping into a warm bath. I began to thaw. My rear end throbbed but my muscles slowed their twitching. My neck began to relax. At some point my testicles might even venture outside. A medic knelt down beside me. He handed me a filthy looking bottle.

"It will warm you. Drink."

I took a small drink and my body tingled from my head to my toes. It was my first taste of vodka. A wave of warmth crashed over me. I took another larger drink and then another. The warmth spread throughout my body. The medic told me to take another drink. I already felt drunk.

"All right, that's enough."

He took the bottle from me. I laid my head down and felt as though I was being spun like a top. I stopped spinning when I felt the medic digging the bullet out of my buttock. It hurt more coming out than going in. I passed out from the pain, vodka and exhaustion.

When I awoke, I started to roll on my back but was quickly reminded why I was lying face down. I was still dizzy and drowsy from the vodka. I was surrounded by other injured soldiers, Russian soldiers.

I was alive but in the bear's den. I was nearly buried alive, almost froze to death and was shot. Now I was alone in a crowd. Would my Russian hold up? I hoped my accent wouldn't betray me either. I had no idea what an authentic Russian accent sounded like. I had never been in Russia before the invasion and spoke Russian as my grandmother spoke it. I could only hope she spoke with an authentic accent and not a Germanized one.

I decided I would speak only when absolutely necessary. Perhaps I could fake an injury to my vocal chords. At least I looked the part of a Russian soldier. Why didn't I join the drama club while in school?! I MUST play the part of a Russian. But what kind of Russian? And from where? My mind raced. I wouldn't be left here for long.

There was no rest for the Russian soldier. Stalin wouldn't allow it. He must be as powerful as Hitler, maybe even more. I feared the Russian campaign failed. We woke a sleeping giant. Our soldiers were better trained but their soldiers seemed to be infinite in number and quickly learned the art of warfare.

They were unbelievably tough men. In one skirmish, one of their soldiers fired at us relentlessly. He was severely wounded. His lower jaw was blown off and he was bleeding profusely but he refused to surrender until a grenade finished him off. The Russian's also had an ally we could not defeat, the Russian Winter.

Hitler became the new Napoleon. History was repeating itself or being plagiarized at least. It was being written with our blood. How much blood would it take to fill the pages? How many would perish? Millions, I suspected. Another great war! I couldn't believe it.

If only we started the campaign a few weeks earlier! We would have made it. I couldn't fathom the number of souls this war was going to consume. Neither Hitler nor Stalin would capitulate. It would be a war of wills. Hitler gambled it all and there was no turning back. He defeated the Allies in the west but did not achieve total victory before striking east. England was kicked out of the house of Europe but the back door was left open.

If we did not defeat Russia with our initial assault we were sure to lose the war. How could the army survive being stretched to its limit across Europe and Russia fighting a two front war? Defeat was only a matter of time. As soldiers, we swore an oath to Hitler not to Germany. As long as he commanded the

Wehrmacht, German soldiers would do their duty and obey his commands. People don't understand this.

There was little dissent in the Wehrmacht. The constant fighting and sub-zero temperatures took its toll but we performed our duty as soldiers. Some may have been opposed to Hitler but none spoke of it.

After he drove the English from the continent, soundly defeated the French and then conquered the rest of Europe, we all believed in his military genius. Now, the bitter cold literally chilled our enthusiasm. Our advance stalled on the outskirts of Moscow. A reconnaissance battalion of 35th Infantry Division of Army Group Center captured a bridge over the Moscow-Volga canal in the Moscow suburb of Khimki. They were 16 kilometers from Moscow. The spires of the Kremlin were in sight!

An armed group of local factory workers and a few available tanks was all it took to repel the farthest advance of the Wehrmacht. Hitler threw a sucker punch at Stalin and now it was Stalin's turn.

What story could I come up with that would be believed? How could I make it back to the Wehrmacht? To Germany? To my family? Russian peasants, farmers and conscripts numbered in the millions. I could blend into their multitude. Yesterday, I was a soldier of the Wehrmacht. Today, I am a novice thespian acting for my life.

As I expected, my rest was soon over. A commissar, political officer, entered the shack and ordered all able-bodied men out. This meant all twelve of us except for the poor soul soon to die. There was a soldier lying on the ground in the back of the hut. A grenade had ripped his gut apart. His intestines poured out of his body and were frozen to him. He made little noise and gently blinked every few seconds.

I got up but fell down when the pain surged through my body as I put weight on my leg. There are a lot of muscles in your rear end! The officer ordered me up and I struggled to my feet. I couldn't lift my right foot to walk so I drug it behind me. I stumbled back out into the horrible cold.

We were a pathetic looking bunch. I was punctured but was in one piece. Three soldiers had head wounds. One of the three was missing an eye. One soldier was missing his left arm. Another had his left arm in a sling. Four soldiers were shot in the leg. The commissar suspected these four soldiers had self-inflicted wounds and treated them with contempt. Two soldiers were badly burned and heavily bandaged. One of the burned had a smooth face. It looked as if it had melted. He now had it covered to protect it from the cold. I saw him in the shack. His nose was gone. Only two gaping holes were left. You could see directly into his face.

We marched to a town named Istra. There was nothing left of it. Istra was burned to the ground as a part of the scorched earth policy issued by Stalin. I remembered how exhausted, frozen and hungry we were when I arrived there days earlier wearing a different uniform. I remembered how my tank crew continually out ran our supply line. There were no winter clothes. We scavenged and stole whatever we could to keep us warm.

There was one Russian soldier here when I arrived with the Wehrmacht. Apparently, he was left behind to stall our advance. He was a teenager, closer to twelve than twenty. He sprung from cover and I shot him in the chest. While he lay dying, a circle of blood grew in diameter beneath him contrasting sharply against the white snow. I didn't give it much thought. I didn't give dying much thought anymore. A soldier ran past me brushing my side. He almost ran past the teen in his haste. He slipped in the snow, threw his carbine aside and sat the boy up.

For a moment I thought he was trying to save him or possibly knew him. I should have known better, especially after experiencing war up close and intimately. He ripped the boy's winter coat off and dropped him back to the blood stained snow. He struggled to put on the coat. It was too small for him but he managed to squeeze into it. The back of the coat was covered with freshly frozen blood. He picked up his carbine and walked away without even looking back. The teenager was still alive. I could see his breath. I walked over to him. He was outstretched as if he were a snow angel. His face was pale. He looked Asian to me. His brown eyes were fixed upon me. I felt pity. It was the first and only time I felt pity during the war. His gaze continued. He was dead. His eyes are what I remember the most.

There is no room for pity in war. It will most certainly get you killed. I wondered if the stealing of the coat brought about that moment of human compassion. My next thought was, 'Why didn't I think of taking the coat for myself?' The pity didn't last long.

Now, I was most certainly a selfish bastard. My only purpose was to survive. I thought achieving victory would save my life. I dreamt of commandeering a warm bed in Moscow. I dreamt of food, lots of food, a beer, warmth and comfort for the victorious army, the Wehrmacht!

We came so close to our objective but I had to stop thinking about it. My mind became so focused. I envisioned Moscow as a finish line. Cross it and we win. It was as if we were mountain climbers only steps away from the summit. How many clichés could I think of? Perhaps the Wehrmacht could regroup and go on the offensive. No, it wasn't meant to be. Let it go. That's easier said than done though. Berlin was now my finish line.

When the Wehrmacht arrived in Istra only half of my company was left after the last four months of fighting. Over half of them were lost to frostbite. One soldier fell asleep while on watch and froze to death standing up. Another died while trying to perform his necessaries. I had no idea it could get so cold. It was as if the wind pushed the warmth out of your body leaving a chattering skeleton and cramping muscles. Now, there was nothing but chaos in Istra. The leveled town was nothing more than disorganized groups of rag tag men. There were many commissars trying to organize companies. How could such an unorganized army throw back the Wehrmacht?

I studied the men's faces. They were dull. They showed no emotion. No panic was drawn upon them. Were these "sub-humans" capable of organized warfare? Germany was the most powerful country in the world. I could not imagine a more well-trained and equipped military. But we were not prepared. We were not prepared for their tenacity or their weather.

How could Hitler be so bold, so reckless? Granted, we were a formidable force. We grew even more so in the previous months of battle. But the feeling in my heart, it was the feeling of impending doom. I couldn't stop feeling that no matter what…the war was lost.

Even if we reached Moscow, we would have to hold it. How? If you asked me in June if we could make it to Moscow, I wouldn't have hesitated and said yes. I believed in the beginning. We took more ground and more prisoners than imaginable. The blitzkrieg was a marvel of modern warfare.

We were stopped but not by opposing forces or because of foul weather. Our advance on Moscow was first stopped by the high command. We were redeployed for other military objectives. After some time, our quest for the capital resumed but we ran out of time. The Russian winter set in. It was the coldest winter in a hundred years. We got so close. The capture of Moscow would have been the Fuhrer's greatest triumph.

But even if we took Moscow the Russians could elude and outnumber us indefinitely. Their massive numbers and the sheer expanse of their country would prevent their defeat.

We were so confident. We thought like the Romans, Alexander the Great and Genghis Khan, we would conquer the world. For the first time, we were stopped and now we were being forced back. It was supposed to be a "Thousand Year Reich". How long would it really last? We made it to the outskirts of Moscow. How far would the Russians make it?

I decided if I could rejoin the Wehrmacht, I would continue to fight for Germany even if defeat were inevitable. For now, I would fight to survive and make it back to my family. I had to play the part of a Russian soldier but I wouldn't kill my fellow countryman. I couldn't bring myself to do that. I would have to think of some way to not kill that wouldn't raise suspicion. Perhaps, I would just be a lousy shot. I would be the worst rifleman in the whole Red Army. I wouldn't be receiving the Order of Lenin for marksmanship, that's for sure. It was a simple plan. It was all I could think of.

How far had Army Group Center been thrown back? What will the Russians do? What is their next objective? What army was I being thrown in with? I soon had one answer.

1st Shock Army. This was to be my Russian army."

Unbelievable

"1st Shock Army?"

"Yes, that is right. 1st Shock Army."

"What is a Shock Army?"

"It is a fast moving army, like our blitzkrieg."

He told me everything in German. I didn't even realize it at first. I guess it was natural for him to express himself in his native tongue.

After much begging and pleading, he finally agreed to tell me about the war. I wanted to ask him a million questions but didn't dare interrupt him. I just wanted him to keep talking.

He didn't tell me about the invasion of the Soviet Union though or the victorious battles that led them to the doorstep of the Russian capital. No, he began with the doorstep.

He began with a pivotal moment for him, the German Army, Germany and the World. The blitzkrieg came to a grinding halt. It was Nazi Germany's first defeat. I couldn't believe what he just told me.

"Grandfather! Are you kidding me? That's the most amazing story I've ever heard!"

"I tell you this on a personal level. You do not write about me. You only use what I tell you to help your studies. Do you understand?"

He was adamant about that. He only agreed to be interviewed if he was not mentioned.

"Yes."

"Do you understand?"

"Yes Sir. I understand."

"I have never talked of these things. It makes me very tired. That is enough for tonight."

"All right Grandfather. Again, thank you. Gute nacht."

"Gute nacht, Enkel."

Enkel? He hadn't referred to me as grandson since I was a little boy.

"Herkommen."

He called to his German Shepard, Blondi, as he walked down the hallway to his bedroom. I'd never seen a more loyal dog. She was very protective of my grandfather. A census taker stopped by my grandfather's house one day. When my grandfather opened the front door Blondi almost ripped the poor man's pants off. It made me uncomfortable that he named her Blondi. Though I'm sure he didn't know it, that's what Hitler named his German Shepard.

How could he know? I'm sure he'd never read a book, watched a TV show or even seen a movie about World War II. Why would he? He lived it. He survived it. He didn't want to reminisce. He didn't want to remember. He didn't want to talk about it. As I locked and pulled the front door shut on my way outside, I wanted to jump up and down for joy. I couldn't believe it. This was actually happening! My grandfather had finally opened up to me.

This was a firsthand account from a German soldier in World War II who was on the front line of the farthest advance of the German Army and the soldier was my own grandfather! This was incredible. I didn't know of any firsthand accounts like this.

There may not be any. And he had a family! I didn't know that. My father probably didn't know either. Did he tell my grandmother?

It was the end of September and the moon was full and bright. It was the harvest moon. It looked huge and I'm sure my eyes were almost as big as it was. As I walked the short distance from his house to the sidewalk, I turned the wrong direction and began walking the wrong way. I was so excited. I almost walked to University Avenue before realizing it. I turned around and starting walking back. I walked past my grandfather's house. All the lights were out. I crossed the street and walked the couple blocks south to Addison's house. I was still in a daze when I walked in the front door. Addison was cooking dinner.

"Well? How'd it go?"

"Incredible! Unbelievable! He has more to tell than I could have ever imagined! And he's a great story teller!"

As we sat eating dinner, I told her about my first interview. I couldn't shut up. I was so excited. I barely ate anything.

I lay in bed staring at the ceiling. I couldn't sleep. Addison was snuggled up to me and lightly snoring. I slithered my way out of bed without waking her. I walked to the kitchen and grabbed a beer from the fridge. I found a lighter and grabbed my hidden pack of cigarettes. Bailey followed me out the back door.

I sat down on the back step and twist the cap off my beer. I took a big gulp and sighed. I pulled out a cigarette and glanced over my shoulder hoping Addison wouldn't be standing there. I was supposed to quit smoking. She would not be pleased to find me out here. I lit the cigarette and took a long, deep drag off it and exhaled slowly. It felt amazing. I hadn't had a cigarette in weeks. A few more puffs and my body began to tingle. As I finished my beer and cigarette, I looked at the moon once more. I was living with the woman I loved and was doing what I loved. It was a great day. I…FELT…GREAT!

The next morning I wanted to head straight back to his house but I didn't. I didn't bother my grandfather for a week. I was dying to hear more. I knew it had been difficult for him to talk about his experience in the war, even if it was just a fraction of the experience he had. I knew this was the tip of the iceberg.

Addison was in love with me but found it strange I was so excited about a German soldier telling me about a war that occurred over half a century ago. She had once referred to him as a Nazi and I about came unglued. I chastised her for not knowing the difference between being a member of the Nazi Party and the Wehrmacht.

"The Nazis were members of a political party. The official name of the party was The National Socialist German Worker's Party. In German, National is pronounced NAZIonal. That's where the name originated. The German Army was called the Wehrmacht. My grandfather was a soldier in the Wehrmacht not a Nazi."

I felt foolish for correcting her. I quickly realized I wasn't correcting her for history's sake but for that of my grandfather. I had endured the grade school taunts of "Your grandfather is a Nazi!" after I made the mistake of telling my classmates about him. It made me mad and defensive. I wanted him to tell me about the war so I could prove to everyone, including myself, that he was not a Nazi. I had no reason to doubt him. My grandfather was the most honest man I knew. "Honest to a fault" is the condition. Pathological honesty is probably a better way to describe it. He always told the truth, no matter what. He was often seen as insensitive. He was not the one to ask if a dress made you look fat.

So, a week later I was able to sit down with him again.

"What about the invasion, Grossvater?"

"What can you tell me about that?"

He seemed distracted.

"Hhm? Oh, yes, the invasion."

Again, he spoke in German.

"It was called Barbarossa. Of course, we didn't know that at the time. We weren't supposed to know anything. But most of us knew something was going on. Something was about to happen, something big. Tanks, trucks and planes were pouring into the east. Everyone was on edge. No one could talk about what was going on but everyone wanted to.

An invasion was imminent. We were young and confident. The Wehrmacht had conquered Europe. How difficult could it be to defeat a nation of sub-humans? That is what we had been taught about the Russians. They were sub-humans occupying land that should belong to the dominant race, the Aryan race, the German people. We were told "No mercy." That is what we showed them and that is what they showed us."

"I was with the 7th Motorcycle Rifle Battalion of the 7th Panzer Division, 39th Motorized Corps, Panzergruppe 3, German Ninth Army of Army Group Center."

"Good grief. How do you remember all that?"

"Some things you never forget."

"I didn't even know you knew how to ride a motorcycle."

"I barely could. I learned to ride one only weeks before the invasion. Luckily, I was assigned a motorcycle with a sidecar. I was in a company that would relay reconnaissance and provide mechanical help to broken down vehicles and tanks. I'm sorry to disappoint you but I have little to tell you about the invasion.

I do remember victory after victory but I was involved in very little of the initial fighting. The Russians were being killed, captured or retreating. It seemed as if the column of captured Russian soldiers marching to Germany was never ending. We were moving so fast the supply trucks couldn't keep up.

Since I had a sidecar, I would go back and forth to take ammunition, supplies and gasoline to the front line. Supplies would be stuffed into and piled on top of the sidecar. If I were to get off the motorcycle the whole thing would fall over. Sometimes I had to recruit a soldier to ride on the passenger seat to balance the weight."

He was a grunt. That's not what I expected. I imagined him as an officer, at least a lieutenant. He definitely had a leadership quality about him.

He continued with more stories about daily life in the army. His experience in war was like any other soldier. There was lack of food, lack of sleep and plenty of stress. It wasn't until the rains began that they were slowed by anything else than the inability of material to keep up.

"It rained and rained and rained. The advance faltered. It wasn't until the first freeze that we were able to start moving again. We slowly made our way closer to Moscow.

The weather chilled dramatically but no winter clothing arrived. I put on every stitch of clothing I had. I was lucky to have my all-weather gear that was issued to motorcycle infantry. The long coat I had was designed to block the wind and rain. I was so glad to have it. I was offered outrageous sums of money for it. My goggles and gauntlet gloves were my next favorite possessions.

It was cold, miserably cold. It was awful. We were moving again but vehicles and tanks began to freeze and wouldn't start. My motorcycle finally succumbed to the freezing weather. I fell in with a tank crew that needed a mechanic.

All I really did was keep the tank engine warm so it wouldn't freeze to death like I thought I was going to. Whenever we stopped, I started a fire underneath the engine to keep it warm. We didn't have enough diesel to run her all the time.

I was lucky to join a tank crew. I knew very little about them as I was trained to work on automobiles but I told no one that. A tank was a tempting target but it was also a shelter. It was worth the risk in my opinion.

The weather worsened but we kept advancing. The Russians kept retreating. They were employing their scorched earth policy and burning anything that might be of use to us. Upon the initial invasion, the Russians were glad to see us. They had suffered under Stalin and the Communists.

When they realized we were not there to improve their lot in life their attitude towards us quickly soured. I didn't care what they thought even at the beginning of the war. Well, you know the rest. We made it within sight of Moscow but got no further."

"Then you became trapped in the snow?"

"Yes, being buried alive scared me more than being shot or blown up."

He sighed heavily.

"I never saw any of my comrades from my tank again. I was the only one to survive."

He sighed again.

"They were excellent soldiers. We became a family. We were fighting for each other and doing everything we could to protect each other. We were fighting to stay alive."

He stopped and stared at the floor.

"Aldous."

"Who?"

"Aldous."

"Who is Aldous? Was he a soldier?"

"Yes. He was a very brave soldier, a very young soldier. He looked older but he was only seventeen."

He paused for a long time. I decided to push him a little. I knew Aldous' fate wasn't good and bothered him to this day but I had to keep him talking.

"What happened to Aldous, grandfather?"

"He was so funny, always joking. He would walk on his hands in the snow. All you could see were a couple of legs sticking up that were moving back and forth.

He could also impersonate anyone. There was an incompetent lieutenant who stuttered horribly and he could mock him perfectly. You couldn't drink around him. He could time his humor just as you were about to take a drink. There were many who had their sinus cavities filled with water, including me."

His smile quickly disappeared. His eyes teared up ever so slightly but he did not cry. I was stunned. This was the most emotion I had ever seen from him.

"The day… the day before our last push on Moscow, he was killed. He was part of the tank crew I joined. When I joined them, they were a tight knit group. It took time for them to accept me. Aldous was the toughest to win over but once I did he was like a brother to me."

He took a deep breath.

"He was walking on his hands and impersonating the stuttering lieutenant at the same time. He could make us forget about the miserable cold and the longing for home at least for a moment. He stood up and smiled at us as we applauded his performance.

The first shell hit him. It was a direct hit. A red bloody mist covered us as the force of the shock knocked us on our butts. We got up and sprinted to the tank and slid underneath it. The shelling seemed like it lasted forever but it was probably less than a minute. Once it stopped, we walked over to where Aldous was standing. There was nothing left of him. A brown dirt crater with a blood red rim surrounded by a sea of white snow replaced poor Aldous where he was standing just moments before."

"Who did you become?" I asked quickly to change the subject.

"Who did I become?"

"Yes. What Russian identity did you take?"

"Oh, that. I called myself Pavel Kruten."

"Why did you choose that name?"

"As a boy, I dreamt of being a fighter pilot in the Great War and flying with Manfred Von Richtofen. You know him as the Red Baron. Everyone in Germany knew who he was. He was our greatest hero. He was credited with 80 air combat victories.

The only Russian names I knew of were the Russian flying aces he faced. The two most notable were Pavel Argeyev and Yevgraph Kruten. They were especially loathed because they served in the French Aeronautique Militaire as well as the Imperial Russian Air Force. They had a paltry 22 kills between them. I kept it simple and merged their names. I told everyone I was from Istra and had been forced from my home by the advancing Germans.

It was doubtful there were any survivors from Istra. If there were, they were retreating to the east as fast as they could. It was the best cover story I could come up with at the spur of the moment. Now, I was a vengeful young peasant ready to fight for Stalin and mother Russia.

I did my best not to become too close to any of the Russian soldiers. I did not want them to inquire about my past and they were still my enemy. They considered me odd and aloof. That was good. I had to be this other person. It was very difficult. My greatest fear was that I would give myself away by speaking German in my sleep."

"That's enough for today."

"All right, Grossvater. Ich danke ihnen."

"You're welcome, Enkel."

Digging Deeper

I was very busy. Spending time with my girlfriend made me very happy. I was working part-time at Eckerd which made me very happy I decided to make a career change. I was trying to get my grandfather to talk as much as possible and I was also training for a sprint triathlon.

I talked Ted into doing the sprint with me. The day of the race, neither of us had a clue as to what we were doing. I still wasn't sure I was even going to make it through the swim when the starting gun fired. I didn't have an actual swimming wetsuit. I used my diving wetsuit which I quickly realized wasn't meant for freestyle swimming. It was very restrictive. Ted bought a wetsuit, the best one on the market. He was never afraid to spend money. He didn't think the swim was that bad. Jerk. We both agreed the water temperature sucked though.

A cold front had blown in the day before. The water temperature was 59 degrees! The outside temperature wasn't much better. It was barely 65 degrees.

The cold water took my breath away. I was shivering and swimming at the same time. I had to back stroke halfway through the swim just so I could breathe without panicking. All my diving experience hadn't prepared me for this. I wasn't ready for the other swimmers either.

People were swimming over me, hitting me and kicking me. My goggles were knocked off. I thought I was in an underwater brawl. Once I was finally out of the water and thanking the dear Lord, I had to transition to the bike. I was experienced with taking off a wetsuit but then trying to put on clothes afterwards was something new.

Try putting on bicycle shorts, a shirt, socks and gloves while you're wet. It was ridiculous. I had left my bicycle shoes clipped into my pedals thinking this would save me some time. Right out of the first transition is a hill. I was trying to get my feet in my shoes before I got to the hill but it took me too long.

As I started up the hill, I lost my momentum and fell over. I was exhausted but had enough energy to be thoroughly embarrassed. The race director helped me up and popped my shoes out of my pedals. He handed them to me.

"You've got hypothermia. Relax. Take your time."

I took some deep breathes, put on my shoes, got back on the bike, clipped in my pedals and started up the hill. The bike wasn't that bad except for climbing the hills in the canyon. On my way back, my legs and lungs were burning. I barely made it up that last hill. I almost got off my bike and walked it up. The run wasn't too bad. I just couldn't get my legs to switch from bicycle mode to run mode. It felt like I had to kick my feet out in front of me.

I did beat Ted out of the water but he passed me on the bike and I couldn't catch him on the run. That fat bastard had bought a new tri bike and flew by me. That's why he beat me. At least, that's what I told myself. My competitive nature was eating at me. I knew I was close to breaking down and buying one of those ridiculously expensive bikes.

I tried to put the agony of defeat behind me and concentrate on my research. I knew my Grandfather could only be coaxed to talk about an hour per interview. I could tell it was draining on him. I wasn't sure why he continued. He didn't have to. I suppose he was just doing it for me. I thanked him profusely.

He started smoking again. He preferred filter-less Lucky Strikes. That's the brand the conquering American soldiers gave him after he surrendered. He stopped smoking when he got married. Evidently, my grandmother did not appreciate this vice. I never knew her though. She died when my father was young. She was from Germany as well. Her family was Jewish and barely survived the war. Some people may find it odd my grandfather married a Jewish woman. He was a German soldier though, not a Nazi. I know the difference.

In between interviews with my Grandfather, I started using the internet. I rarely used the internet even when I was in pharmacy school. I was amazed at the amount of information on it about World War II and the Nazis. I had no idea how much the internet had grown since public use of the World Wide Web began in 1993. Apparently, it wasn't just used to post a sex tape of your ex-wife.

Simon Wiesenthal, the greatest Nazi hunter of them all, had a website. The amount of information he had on file was amazing. If I couldn't find it in the library or on the internet, I would consult Dr. Biterman. I'm sure his collection of documents was only rivaled by Wiesenthal's.

Dr. Biterman hated the internet. He didn't trust anything on it. He had seen documents on it that he could prove were altered and there were a number of sites that purported the Holocaust was a hoax. He was livid the day he saw one of these. He had every right to be. His entire family was murdered during the Holocaust.

I never brought up anything I found on the internet. It wasn't worth the tirade that would ensue. He would let me look at his stacks and stacks of papers, reports and pictures in his cramped office. His office was a mess. He could barely get to his desk. He wouldn't allow me to take anything out of his office. I had to wheel a copy machine in the doorway to make copies. He didn't want to lose anything.

His research was precious to him but he would share it with anyone truly interested in history and someone he trusted. Luckily, I was both. It wasn't near as hard for me to gain access to his vault as it was to convince my grandfather to share his memories. I hadn't asked Dr. Biterman about his experience during the war as he had shared almost all of it during his lectures. I knew there were things he hadn't shared and didn't want to because they were too personal and too painful.

Dr. Biterman was pushing me to come up with a thesis. It wasn't very original but I did have a general idea for my thesis. In a nutshell, it was genocide from a to z, birth of an idea to the death of millions.

The Nazis didn't invent it but Germany is the only modern country with an educated and sophisticated society to engage in the deliberate mass murder of a people. The sheer scale of the Holocaust is hard to comprehend.

It was a different world at that time in history and I understand that. But how was it so different that something like the Holocaust could possibly have happened? I wanted to explore the German culture, timing of world events, the world view of Jews, anti-Semitism, and the hangover of World War I that contributed to the foundation of the Holocaust. There is no one explanation for the largest crime in history but I wanted to provide a plausible explanation for the culmination of factors that could make such a thing a reality.

Dr. Biterman just stared at me. He was expressionless. I thought I was going to piss my pants. I just told the professor I respected more than any other that I wanted to objectively evaluate the thing that killed his entire family. He walked past his stacks of papers and sat down at his desk.

"All right."

He began dissecting another student's paper with his infamous red pen. Dr. Biterman loved using it to make corrections and dismiss novice historians' work as tawdry. I slowly backed out of his office and headed to my grandfather's house.

I had told Dr. Biterman about my grandfather. He was taken aback. I explained what my grandfather's experience was like in the war and that he had no part in any of the atrocities that occurred. I emphasized that he only fought the Russians. I thought since the Russians had occupied half of Poland after the war started he would hate the Russians almost as much as the Nazis.

It didn't matter what I told Dr. Biterman. He didn't care. To him, any German soldier was a Nazi. No one or thing was going to change his opinion of that. I had thought about introducing the two of them but now I was absolutely sure it was a bad idea. There was too much history there.

Dr. Biterman wouldn't meet my grandfather but I knew how important it was to continue the interviews. My grandfather's stories continued to amaze me. He was at Stalingrad AND the Battle of Kursk. It was at Stalingrad that my grandfather was able to rejoin the Wehrmacht. He told me how during his next interview.

"The Wehrmacht controlled 90 percent of the city. The Russians desperately held onto a one kilometer strip of land along the Volga River. It looked like it would only be a matter of weeks before Stalingrad was in German hands and the oil fields in the Caucuses could provide desperately needed fuel. Then the Wehrmacht could push to Moscow and make it there before the weather turned to crap again.

The fighting was street to street, house to house and room to room. Snipers were inflicting casualties. Stuka dive bombers were constantly attacking. I realized in this utter chaos, I might be able to separate myself from the Russians and rejoin the Wehrmacht. If I didn't, I would be killed with the Russians or taken prisoner by my own countrymen and executed for being a traitor.

I volunteered to lead a patrol. It was suicidal to take point at Stalingrad. I led the patrol into a factory that had changed hands numerous times. As we entered the factory, bomber engines roared overhead. I took cover under a desk as a bomb fell into the middle of the factory. Glass and metal fell from the ceiling as the bomb exploded. Men were cut in half and impaled. I heard the order to fall back but stayed under the desk.

I remained there until the survivors left the factory. I crawled out from under the desk and surveyed my surroundings. Smoke and dust filled the factory. I made my way to the west end of the factory and crouched behind what was left of a wall. I was now literally between two armies.

Suddenly, I heard German voices on the other side of the wall. I was still in a Russian uniform! I had to think fast. I threw my rifle away and took off all my clothes. I then called to the soldiers.

"Nicht schiessen! Nicht schiessen!"

"Zeige dich! Zeige dich schnell!"

I told them not to shoot and I showed myself as ordered. I slowly stood up and extended my arms around the wall. I took a deep breath and stepped out from behind the wall.

"Why the hell are you naked?"

"I was taking a bath."

"A bath? In the middle of all this hell? You're nuts!"

I fell in with a company but never told anyone about my harrowing journey to that point. I was afraid they would accuse me of being a traitor. I was overjoyed to be free of the Russians and with my army. My joy didn't last long. The matter of weeks passed and the tide of the battle turned in favor of the Russians."

The German Sixth Army under General Friedrich von Paulus was encircled by the Russians. Paulus had lost 150,000 men since the battle commenced. The remaining 91,000 soldiers were freezing, starving and running out of ammunition. It was a dire situation. Paulus requested a tactical retreat. Hitler forbade it.

Hermann Goring, the pompous Reichminister of Aviation, convinced Hitler he could save the Sixth Army. His resupply effort from the air failed miserably. Field Marshall Erich von Manstein mounted a rescue mission but the weather would not permit it. The Sixth Army probably could have fought their way out. Instead, they were ordered to hold their ground at all costs.

Hitler promoted Paulus to Field Marshall and Paulus understood what this meant. His soldiers understood what this meant as well. No Field Marshall had ever been captured or surrendered. Hitler expected Paulus to command his troops to the last man and then commit suicide. Paulus refused to sacrifice the lives still under his command or take his own. The recently promoted Field Marshall surrendered. Hitler was absolutely livid.

"Death would have been better than to surrender to the Russians. I knew what I had to do. It was the hardest thing I've ever done. I knew how we treated Russian prisoners, so did the Russians. They were exacting their revenge and treating German prisoners even worse.

Returning to the Russians as one of them was my only hope of survival. I found and stripped the frozen corpse of a Russian soldier and again donned a Russian uniform as I had first done in that Russian tank a year ago. I weaved my way through the rubble that was Stalingrad and joined a front line company as my Russian self. I was not happy to re-enlist."

He was right. Out of approximately 91,000 soldiers taken prisoner, roughly 5,000 returned to Germany after the war.

"After Stalingrad, I was able to finagle my way into a tank crew given my mechanical aptitude. The Russian tanks were crap compared to ours but I quickly learned how to work on them. When the driver was killed, I inherited a second job. Now I was responsible for maintaining and driving the tank. The following summer we took part in the Battle of Kursk. I can't tell you much about the battle though.

When it began I could see Panzer and Tiger tanks coming at us from all directions. After an hour of fighting on the first day, I could barely see anything. The smoke from the battle was as thick as fog. It was absolute chaos. I listened to the tank commander and did whatever he told me. We could have driven off a cliff and I would have never seen it coming. We raced back and forth to get fuel and ammunition. Tanks were blowing up and shells were exploding all around us but we weren't hit once.

The only time we stopped, ate, or performed our necessaries was when we stopped to refuel and reload. The only time we slept was when our tank commander passed out from exhaustion while we were behind the front line. The battle lasted from the beginning of July to the end of August. When the battle finally ended, my hands wouldn't stop shaking and my ears rang for two days. My nerves were shot. That horrific winter on the outskirts of Moscow was the only thing worse than the Battle of Kursk."

The Battle of Kursk is the largest tank battle in history. Almost 2,000 tanks were engaged in the battle. Germany lost 350 tanks on the very first day. By the end of the battle they lost a total of 700 tanks and 50,000 soldiers. It was the last major German offensive of the war.

My grandfather had been everywhere. He had been a part of two of the most historic battles of World War II, two of the most historic battles ever! Was he going to wind up in Hitler's bunker at the end of the war? My grandfather was turning into the Forrest Gump of World War II.

I could feel the stress it caused my grandfather to talk about the war. I knew he wasn't going to tell me much more. It was too hard on him even if it was cathartic. I did need to know more though. What was the fate of his family? How did he manage to survive and surrender to the allies without being discovered by the Russians?

Execution Tourists

"Wherever they burn books, they will also, in the end, burn human beings." - Heinrich Heine, German poet

I made a lot of progress on my thesis. I examined the world of the early twentieth century and gained an understanding or at least came to realize that dislike and mistrust of Jews did exist. Anti-Semitism was not isolated to Nazi Germany. It was prevalent in Europe and America. Prior to the war, there were many Nazi sympathizers. Some were even famous and influential. The Duke and Duchess of York were Nazi supporters. Prominent Americans such as Henry Ford and Charles Lindbergh were anti-Semites. Lindbergh had visited Nazi Germany to inspect the Luftwaffe. Hitler was a fan of both men. Hitler even said, "You can tell Herr Ford that I am a great admirer of his." It was indeed a different world then.

Anti-Semitism was present in Germany well before the Nazis came to power. However, it was something they expanded upon exponentially. The Jews were an easy scapegoat. Hitler said, "If the Jew had not existed, we would have had to invent him." A common enemy provided a common bond for the German people. Distrust of the Weimar Republic that signed the absurd Treaty of Versailles was another. The treaty was foolish of the victors. If Germany had been rebuilt and accepted back into the community of modern countries, all of this may have been averted. That's my opinion any way. Dr. Biterman concurred.

Germany felt isolated. The German people didn't trust America or the other European countries. They were fearful of a Communist revolution. The Nazis promised to protect Germans from the threat of Communism while snubbing their noses at the Treaty of Versailles.

Then the stock market crashed and the German economy was ruined. Over 4 million Germans were unemployed. The Nazis now promised work and bread.

The Nazi Party anti-Semitic rhetoric did not fall on deaf ears but did not prompt any wide-scale popular criticism. Nazis considered Jews to be the common enemy but political rivals had to be dealt with first.

Political opponents were the first inhabitants of concentration camps. The next were anyone the Nazis wanted out of the way. Homosexuals, Gypsies and Jews joined the political prisoners. Murder had not become a mainstay of concentration camps as it is directly associated with today. Aside from the murder of political rivals in the streets by the SA (the Sturmabteilung or Storm Detachment) who were more commonly known as brownshirts because of their brown uniforms, the Nazi's had started murdering elsewhere.

Their euthanasia program began with the mentally handicapped. The Nazi belief in survival of the fittest and racial hygiene did not mesh with the care of mental patients. Erbliche Belastung (hereditary taint) was not acceptable to the Nazis. They saw no reason to care for those considered useless to the state and the longevity of the Aryan race. Sterilization was the first step. Euthanasia soon followed. Mental patients were considered "defectives", "useless eaters" and "incurables". Their lives were not considered worth living. Nazi logic was "Why bother sterilizing them when their pitiful lives could be ended humanely?" In their sick minds, they could say they were doing the patients, their families and Germany a service.

The Germans under Nazi rule may have tolerated or dismissed anti-Semitic policies instituted but the euthanasia of mental patients raised public outcry. The Nazis had gone too far for Germans. The euthanasia programs were cancelled, at least publicly. Soon, the programs started up again but this time in secret. Families were notified that patients had fallen ill and died from common medical complications such as a burst appendix. Many families were skeptical, especially those of patients who already had their appendixes removed.

In reality, most of the victims were killed by lethal injections. The Nazis experimented with other methods as well. Mobile killing vans were soon employed. The exhaust pipes of enclosed vehicles were routed into the back cargo areas. Victims were locked in these vehicles and the engine would run. The exhaust killed those trapped inside. The first gas chambers were mobile.

Jews still remained the focus of Nazi hatred though. Kristallnacht, or Night of the Broken Glass, was a clear indicator of Nazi intent. On the night of August 23, 1938 a total of 267 synagogues were burned, 7,500 Jewish owned businesses and homes were destroyed and 91 Jews were murdered. Over 30,000 Jews, mainly young men, were imprisoned. Those arrested were transferred to concentration camps. Kristallnacht was an elevated level of Nazi persecution of the Jews.

Once the war began, it was easy for the Nazis to target the Jews. This was the next major factor to accelerate the beginning of the Holocaust. Land captured in the east, especially Poland, was prime real estate for the establishment of concentration camps. Jews from the conquered countries of Europe were sent there. As many men, women and children as possible were crammed into cattle cars. As many cars as could be pulled by a train engine were hooked up and headed east. Those who survived the journey were put to work. The construction of gas chambers and crematoria began. Then came the invasion of the Soviet Union.

"When Barbarossa begins, the world will hold its breath."
- Adolf Hitler

Hitler was right. On June 22, 1941, the invasion began. Hitler always planned on invading the Soviet Union. One only needs to read Mein Kampf (one of the worst books ever written by the way) to know this. Lebensraum, living space in the east for Germany to expand, was one of his essential goals for Germany. Hitler was convinced that without expansion into Eastern Europe, Germany would become stagnant as a nation and grow weak in comparison to the Western powers. In his mind, conquest in Eastern Europe would ensure the survival and proliferation of Germany. Germany would then be poised for world domination. For Hitler, it was vital.

Hitler chose to ignore his own advice he penned in Mein Kampf. He believed the cardinal error in the conquest of the Soviet Union was an attack while engaged in a Western front. He should have heeded his own advice. He was right. Great Britain had been forced across the English Channel but was not defeated.

At the time of the invasion, the Red Army was massive. It had as many aircraft, tanks and reserves of manpower as the rest of the world combined. It was a formidable foe. It did have one major weakness though. It's Achilles' heel was lack of leadership. With his purges, Stalin had decimated the officer corps to strengthen his control of the Soviet Union.

He accomplished his goal but weakened his army and left the Soviet Union vulnerable to defeat if any country were mad enough to invade. Enter Nazi Germany. Per Hitler, "You have only to kick in the door and the whole rotten structure will come crashing down."

The invasion proceeded better than even Hitler expected. It seemed as though the campaign was running itself. Most of the Generals and the army as a whole thought the war would be over in a matter of weeks.

Vilnius, Lithuania, which is over 1,000 kilometers from Berlin, was captured on June 24th, two days after the invasion began! June 24th is also the day Napoleon took Vilnius. This fact did not slip by General Franz Halder. He remarked that it was an "ominous coincidence".

Colonel Bernd von Kleist equated the German army as an elephant attacking a host of ants. He wrote:

…The elephant will kill thousands, perhaps even millions of ants, but in the end their numbers will overcome him and he will be eaten to the bone…

There was a different kind of animal behind the elephant, the SS.

On the Eastern Front, things were different. It was an ideological war. It was a war of annihilation. Europeans were considered human. Russians were not. They were considered sub-human as the Jews were. A Russian Jewish Communist did not stand a chance. Hitler ordered Jews, party officials, and others considered an immediate threat to be killed on the spot. Concentration camps and work programs were not needed for these people. Working behind the front lines and following Hitler's orders were the Einsatzgruppen. Their official name was Einsatzgruppen der Sicherheitspolizei und des Sicherheitsdienst which translates to Task Forces of the German Secret Police and Security Service.

They were mobile killing squads. That's all they were. They weren't sent to fight the Russians. Their task was murder. Their job was to murder those perceived to be racial or political enemies and most importantly kill Jews. The Einsatzgruppen were composed solely of SS soldiers. Some of these soldiers already had experience killing. The euthanasia program instituted for mental patients had been started and run by the SS. These soldiers were familiar with death. Some Einsatzgruppen were as large as battalions. This is where the full-scale killing of Jews began.

There was so much information on the internet and in Dr. Biterman's office that I felt like I was going cross-eyed from reading so much. I had constant headaches and was exhausted. I was working, doing research and trying to spend quality time with my girlfriend. Addison had been accepted into pharmacy school and was busy with her studies. As if I didn't have enough going on in my life, I decided to sign up for the half Ironman, the Ironman 70.3 at Buffalo Springs Lake. I even managed to talk Ted into signing up for it. I vowed to beat him this time, even if I had to buy an outrageously expensive tri bike.

When I was too tired to read, I would study photographs. There weren't many pictures of the Holocaust. It stands to reason; most soldiers didn't want to be recorded committing atrocities. Some didn't seem to mind and some even smiled in photographs. They were as hard to look at just as the accounts of the Holocaust were to read. "A picture is worth a thousand words" is an old phrase and it is certainly true. But these pictures say more than a thousand words.

Dr. Biterman had more photographs of atrocities being committed during the Holocaust than I had been able to find on the internet. Those clandestinely taken by prisoners or resistance fighters were often blurry and captured only part of a scene. Pictures taken by sadistic soldiers were the least blurry and better quality. The soldiers foolish enough to have their pictures taken were the easiest to find after the war. The partisans referred to them as "execution tourists".

Dr. Biterman had done much research on the Einsatzgruppen. I realized my idea for a thesis was too broad and I needed to narrow my focus in order to develop a viable thesis topic. I decided to concentrate my research on the Einsatzgruppen. Dr. Biterman approved.

The Einsatzgruppen quickly developed different methods of murder. At first, prisoners were shot in the back of the head at the base of the skull. This was the most effective place for a bullet to strike and it was less psychologically stressful on the soldier because they did not have to look their victims in the face. This was quickly considered to be highly inefficient. Efficient methods were soon developed though.

Prisoners were arranged single file, all facing the same direction. An executioner would stand behind the prisoner in the back of the line. He would shoot the prisoner at point blank range. One bullet would usually pass through up to three prisoners, thus saving bullets and the executioner still did not have to look his victims in the face. This process would continue until the last prisoner in line had been shot. When machine guns were available, victims were simply mowed down.

Children were usually beaten to death. The reason was two fold. One was simply to save bullets. The other was experience. Bullets easily passed through a child's body. A ricochet could injure or kill a soldier. Small children were held at the ankles and soldiers swung them head first into a wall or other solid object.

If this could possibly be any worse, the children were killed first so their mothers could witness it before being killed themselves. There are reports of SS soldiers using the bodies of small children to beat the mothers to death. Pregnant women were kicked or shot in the abdomen to kill their unborn child before they too were murdered. There is one report of a German soldier walking down the street with a year-old baby impaled on his bayonet. The baby was still alive and crying weakly. The German was singing. Horrific.

Mass killings with mass graves soon began. The Red Army forced local populations to dig trenches in a desperate attempt to slow the Nazi assault. These trenches dug as defensive positions were highly ineffective and came to serve a much different purpose. Unbeknownst to them, these victims had dug their own graves.

Natural ravines were used as well. Prisoners were forced to stand or kneel at the edge. They would be shot in the back of the head and fall into a ravine or pit. As described earlier, the more efficient Einsatzgruppen would line the victims in rows and shoot them to save bullets.

Those yet to die would throw the bodies in. Small children and elderly that would not be able to climb out on their own were thrown in. The most infamous mass killing of this sort occurred at Babi Yar. This is a ravine located northwest of Kiev, Ukraine. At Babi Yar, more than 30,000 Jews were massacred over the course of two days in September of 1941.

The most efficient groups would use a method called Sardinenpackung which is exactly what it sounds like. At first, they would shoot the victims and have other prisoners stack their bodies into rows as if they were sardines in a can.

Later on, the victims were instructed to lie upon each other in layers of two. The victim on top would be shot and if lined up correctly the victim lying underneath would die from the same bullet.

This process was repeated in layers of humans. If those below were not shot, it did not particularly matter because after the executions were complete and there was no more room in the pit the victims yet to die would cover the pit with dirt. Those in the pit who may not have been shot or were shot and still alive were trapped. They were buried alive. There were a few victims who were able to climb out of this sea of corpses and miraculously survived. Their stories are proof of these atrocities.

The last to be executed in these "aktions" were Jews deemed to be wealthy. Their body orifices were first searched for jewels and anything of value before being murdered.

The number of Jews and undesirables to be killed soon exceeded the availability of space for their corpses. Those to be killed were in no hurry to dig their own graves. Dynamiting craters was used to excavate mass graves.

When they ran out of dynamite, the mass graves full of corpses were soaked with fuel and set ablaze to make room for more and at the same time destroy evidence of their appalling crimes. Some of the victims forced to perform these tasks were driven mad by the horror before them and jumped into the flames.

Once the charred remains settled in the pits, the next group of victims was executed. This process continued until there was no more room and the site was covered with dirt. Fuel was needed for the war effort so another method had to be found.

Quicklime, calcium oxide, was chosen as the replacement. A process called "slaking of the lime" was used. Slaking of the lime is adding water to calcium oxide which causes a chemical reaction forming a strong acid, calcium hydroxide. This is the same acid found in concentrated household bleach. Slacking of the lime greatly sped up the rate of decomposition.

The quicklime was spread over the bodies during the executions. Layer after layer of quicklime was spread over the bodies until the mass grave was at capacity. Water was then poured over the bodies and calcium hydroxide was produced. Inevitably, not all of the victims were dead. What occurred next was deemed by the Nazi high command to be too stressful even for the most sadistic and barbaric of the Einsatzgruppen.

The chemical reaction that occurs is exothermic and produces a great deal of heat. Those still alive were chemically burned to death as the calcium hydroxide dissolved their tissues. The screams of those being boiled alive are unimaginable. The soldiers ripped pieces of cloth from the victims' discarded clothing and stuffed them in their ears to block out the cries of those dying and those waiting their turn. Once the liquefied mass of human remains collapsed to the bottom, the process was repeated. The high command ordered the use of quicklime to be stopped.

These constant killing sprees had psychological effects on the soldiers committing them. Even the "master race" was not immune to this utter loss of humanity. Many turned to alcohol to numb their conscience and strengthen their resolve. They knew if they lost the war and their actions were discovered they would all have to pay for this.

The most efficient and least taxing method of extermination was being developed in the concentration camps. A killing and disposal method was being developed to handle the increasing number of undesirables from all corners of the third Reich arriving at the camps every day. Massive gas chambers and crematoria were the final solution.

I asked my grandfather about the Einsatzgruppen, concentration camps and the Holocaust. He, as almost the whole of Germany, knew nothing of the atrocities occurring. The greatest crime ever committed was well hidden.

A Resemblance

A ddison and I were at the library. She was studying and I was annoying her. She had enough and told me to leave her alone so I walked over to the History building to see if Dr. Biterman was working. He usually worked in the evenings and tonight was no exception. I poked my head in his office and knocked on the doorframe. He glanced up to see me.

"Rick, my good friend and student! Come in. Come in."

He was as friendly as usual.

"Mind if I do a little research?"

"Not at all. Be my guest."

More like good luck. His office seemed messier than usual. I pulled a stack of photographs out of one of the many cardboard boxes that were stacked around his desk.

"Oh, Rick!"

He startled me and I dropped the stack of pictures.

"Sorry, Professor. You nearly gave me a heart attack."

I knelt on the floor and began picking up the pictures.

I could tell he was not happy with me.

"What were you going to say?"

"I don't remember. Please be very careful with the photographs."

"Yes Sir."

One picture slid under his desk. I had to get down on my hands and knees and crawl under the desk to retrieve it. It was filthy down there. I don't think Dr. Biterman had ever cleaned his office. I stood up and blew the dust off the photo. I suddenly felt very nauseated.

"Rick? Are you OK? You're as white as a ghost."

He pulled out a chair for me.

"Sit down dear boy. What's wrong?"

I handed him the photograph. He looked at it and back at me.

"What is it Rick?"

"The man on the edge of the photograph, he looks like me."

Dr. Biterman held the picture close and squinted.

"My dear boy, there is an unfortunate resemblance but there is nothing to get upset about."

I motioned for the professor to pass the picture to me.

"Could I look at it again?"

"Sure. Sure."

He handed me the photograph.

"I'll get you a glass of water."

I stared at the face of the soldier in the picture. He looked like me. My hand was shaking. I sat the picture down on his desk.

"Here."

He handed me a glass of water and I took a few sips. He looked at me still concerned. I tried to smile and play it off.

"Weird, huh? Threw me for a loop. I'm sorry Professor. I've been working too hard. Not enough sleep, you know."

"Mind if I make a copy to show Addison? She won't believe it either."

"Sure. I'll get the copier."

I drank some more water. He rolled in the copy machine.

"Hand me the picture."

I retrieved the picture from his desk and handed it to him. He quickly placed it face down on the copier. He handed the warm copy to me. I folded the copy carefully as not to crease the picture, especially the face of the soldier who I unfortunately resembled. I felt strong enough to stand. I stretched my hand out to the professor. He did the same and we shook hands.

"I better go get Addison. She's studying at the library."

"OK, Rick. Have a good rest of the evening."

"You too. See you tomorrow."

I walked back to the library and got Addison. She was tired of studying and ready to go home. We hopped in my truck and I drove her home. I pulled up to the house to let her out.

"Aren't you coming in?"

"No."

"Where are you going?"

"I'm going to see if my grandfather is still up."

"Rick, it's late. I know you're tired and your grandfather is probably asleep already."

"Yes, I am and he may be asleep but I've got a few questions I've thought of to ask him. It shouldn't take long."

"OK. Please don't take too long."

"I promise."

"OK. Love you."

"Love you."

I made the short drive to his house. I pulled up and saw the living room light was still on. He answered the door and surprisingly agreed to another interview at this late hour.

"How did the war end for you grandfather?"

"In Berlin."

"How did you make it back to Berlin?"

"I fell in with Marshal Georgy Zhukov's army. Everyone knew he would be leading the final assault on Berlin. He saved Moscow and Stalingrad. He would now conquer Berlin. The battle began on April 20th. Stalin chose this date deliberately. It was Hitler's birthday.

The defense of the city was pathetic. Old men and boys were the only ones left to defend the Third Reich. Along with the Russian Army, I was within the city limits of Berlin. I prayed Lena, Magda and Ulrich had made it out of Berlin. If not, I prayed they were safe."

"How did you expect to find them?"

"All I could do was make my way to our flat. I didn't know where else to look. I had nowhere else to look. I didn't even know if our flat was still there. Berlin had been shelled for days."

"What did you do?"

"I waited until dusk then separated from my company. I crawled through rubble and remains of buildings and around broken down vehicles and corpses. I saw Hitler youth running around with panzerfaust, crude but effective bazookas, ready and willing to take on any Russian tank. I managed to get within two blocks of our flat."

I suddenly realized how bad my grandfather looked. He looked horrible and was slurring his words. I noticed a bottle of cheap whiskey next to his recliner. He was drunk. I had never seen him drunk.

"I was two blocks away when a bullet hit the ground just in front of me. I dropped to the ground and took cover. I slowly made my way closer to our flat. I knew it was not a sniper. His aim was not good enough. I took my helmet off and moved it into a vulnerable position. He took another shot. I knew where he was now. He was on the third floor, the same floor as our flat. I took my time and lined up my shot. I moved the helmet with my foot. He fired again. I had him. I fired.

I made my way into the building and upstairs where he had taken his position. He lay there as if he were ready to take another shot. But there was no way I missed. I told him to take his hands off the rifle. He didn't move. I kicked his boot and he moaned. I had hit him. I put my rifle to the back of his head, knelt down and grabbed his rifle. I threw it away and stood up. I told him to roll over. He did not move. He only moaned.

I placed my left leg along the right side of his body and used it to roll him over as I kept my rifle on him. He was dying. I could see it in his eyes and he knew I was the one who pulled the trigger."

"Did you then make it to the flat?"

"Yes."

"Did you find them?"

"Lena and Magda were there."

"Well? What happened?"

"They had been raped by the Russians. Magda was in her bedroom. She was dead. There was a knife in her right hand and her left wrist was cut. She had taken her life after being raped over and over again. My little girl…"

He closed his eyes and covered his mouth. He took a couple of deep breaths and continued.

"Lena would soon join her. She had been raped and severely beaten. She lay behind the couch on the living room floor.

I terrified her. Her eyes were almost completely swollen shut and she could barely see. She could only recognize the Russian uniform.

I took off my helmet and knelt down beside her. I told her to listen to my voice.

"Lena, my love, it's Friedrich. I'm here. It's really me."

She realized it was me and tears ran down her face. She began to speak but I could barely hear her. I wrapped my arms around her and held her tight. I loosened my grip and turned my ear to her mouth.

"You're alive. You're alive. I can't believe it. Thank God you're alive."

"Yes, I'm alive and I found you. You're safe now."

She quietly sobbed as I rocked her back and forth. I relaxed my arms and laid her down. She weakly smiled and exhaled for the last time. She was dead. They were all dead. I was too late."

"Wait. What about Ulrich?"

"He was dead too."

"When did you find him?"

"I shot him. He was the novice sniper. He was trying to protect his mother and sister. He lived long enough to recognize me. He shook his head back and forth. He couldn't believe it was me, that I was in a Russian uniform and I was the one who shot him. I dropped my rifle and knelt down beside him. I yelled "No!" over and over again. I pulled him to my chest and held him tightly. His head fell back and his arms dropped to the ground. He was dead. I killed my son."

"Grandfather...I am so sorry. Please forgive me. I should never have asked you to tell me these things."

"It's all right. It is good to get these things off my chest. War is terrible, absolutely terrible."

"It's not all right. I had no right. You survived the war and put all this horror behind you. I made you do this. I'm sorry. I'm so sorry."

"You did not know. You have helped me accept what happened. It has taken many years for me to talk of such things. I feel better now that I have."

"What about the picture?"

"Picture? What picture?"

I reached into my pocket and pulled out the copy of the picture Dr. Biterman made for me. I handed it to him.

"This picture."

The Fall

He unfolded the paper and carefully studied the picture. It was an old photograph. The corners were torn off as if it had been taped in a photo album and ripped out. It had been folded and some of the faces were unrecognizable because of the creases. His face was recognizable though.

He is only partially in the picture. The left part of his body is cropped out of the photograph. His head is just below the torn corner. If another half inch had been ripped off he would not be identifiable. They are in uniform but it is not a wartime photograph. He is wearing a Captain's uniform.

"Father told me he had seen pictures of you when you were about my age. He said we were the spitting image of each other. I believe the German word is doppelganger."

His demeanor suddenly changed. He leaned back in his recliner. Blondi walked up to him and sat beside his chair waiting for him to pet her. He ignored her. She pawed at him.

"Nein. Not now Blondi."

Blondi sulked away into the kitchen.

"Yes, I can see the resemblance. I have never seen this photograph. I don't remember it being taken."

He sat the copy next to his drink.

"Where did you find it?"

"Dr. Biterman has it."

"Does he know who is in it?"

"Do you mean does he know you are in it?"

"Yes, that is precisely what I mean."

"Nein."

He glared at me.

"I cannot change the past. There was a war. I was a soldier and I did my duty."

"You're wearing an SS uniform in the picture. All the men in the picture are wearing SS uniforms."

"Pretzsch."

"What?"

"The picture. It is from Pretzch."

"What is Pretzch?"

"It is a town on the Elbe River. It is about eighty kilometers southwest of Berlin."

"We were ordered to report there for training."

"Who was?"

"We were, the SS, thousands of us."

"What did you do there?"

"I volunteered and was accepted into the SS. My commander told me I was needed for an important operation because I could speak Russian. He told me it would be very dangerous. I agreed without hesitation. There were many of us there who could speak Russian."

"We were organized into Einsatzgruppen."

I leapt into the air.

"Einsatzgruppen! The SS! Are you serious!?"

"You murdered people!"

"You weren't a soldier! You were a murderer!"

"I was a soldier! I was trained and I did my duty! That's it. It's that simple. Whether what I did was right or wrong, just or unjust doesn't matter. War is hell. There are no rules. We lost the war and then there were rules. Then we were blamed for everything."

"What about your story? The one you told me. It's not true, is it?

"It is true. It is true but not for me."

"What do you mean?"

"I was never behind enemy lines. The few of us still alive made it back to Berlin as the city was being shelled. I left what remained of my Einsatzgruppen. I was trying to get to the west so I could surrender to the Americans. The shelling was relentless. I managed to take cover in a flat that was partially collapsed.

There was a soldier in there. I didn't see him when I first crawled into it. I got inside and quickly turned around to see if anyone had seen me. I sat down with my back against the wall and closed my eyes. I probably would have fallen asleep from exhaustion but I heard him speak."

"Nicht schiessen bitte."

"He said it weakly. My eyes popped open. I glanced around the room but did not see anyone. I saw a boot sticking out from behind the couch. It wasn't a German boot. I slowly crept around the other end of the couch. I quickly glanced behind the couch. There lay a woman and a man. The woman was a bloody mess.

Her clothes were almost completely ripped off. She wasn't moving. I was certain she was dead. I could slowly see his chest rise and fall. He was alive but barely. He was holding his abdomen. His shirt was soaked with blood. It was a mortal wound. He was wearing a Russian uniform. I did not see a weapon."

"Russki?"

"Nein."

I crept back to the front of the couch and moved to the other end. Again, I glanced around the back of the couch and spoke to him.

"Are you German?"

"Yes."

"Why are you wearing that uniform?"

"It's a long story"

"Why don't you go ahead and tell it."

I stared at my grandfather. I didn't understand.

My grandfather could see I was confused.

"It was his story, the dying German soldier in the Russian uniform."

"You told me his story?"

"Yes. He was the one who was almost buried alive in the snow on the outskirts of Moscow. He was the one who hid amongst the Russians. He was the one at Stalingrad and at Kursk. He was the one who did it all to get back to his family. He was the one who shot and killed his son, found his daughter raped and dead and found his wife raped and dying. It was his story, not mine. The only part that isn't true is he didn't survive. He died there lying next to what was left of his wife. It is true that he shot and killed his son but his son had shot him as well. The father outlived the son only by a few hours, only long enough to tell me his story. I committed his story to memory in case I ever needed it."

"So, what is your story? What did you do?"

"Exactly what you think I did."

"That poor bastard had been on the front lines of Army Group Center that pushed on Moscow whereas I was in the Einsatzgruppen that followed Army Group Center."

My grandfather picked up the picture and studied it again.

"We had spent three weeks in Pretzch training. We knew what was going on. We were going to invade the Soviet Union. We were never told this but everyone knew what was happening.

The training was intended to harden us to the tasks we would have to carry out. We sat through lectures on honor, duty, the superiority of the Aryan race and the subhuman Mongols we were about to attack. We watched propaganda films about the Jews and Russians. There was little actual military training.

We were only told a few days before the invasion began that we were going to Russia. I was assigned to Einsatzgruppe B under SS-Brigadefuhrer Arthur Nebe attached to Army Group Center. We were ordered to protect the rear army area and quell any resistance. We were told to "pacify" the enemy.

Nebe spoke to us before the invasion. He instructed us to conquer any weakness inside of us, that each man must do this to accomplish the task at hand. Ours was a task necessary for the survival of the German people. Only the strongest Germans, those who had joined the ranks of the SS were capable of completing this task. He said, 'In life, sometimes violence is necessary. This is a necessary violence in this life.' "

"I feel sick."

"I am sorry Enkel. I did not want you to know of these things. I wanted to protect you from the truth as I have protected myself all these years. I think about it every day. Every day I wonder if I will be discovered."

I got up and walked into the kitchen. Blondi was lying in front of the refrigerator. I reached into the cabinet beside the sink and got a small glass. I returned to the living room and picked up the bottle of whiskey on the floor beside my grandfather's chair. I filled the glass half full and took a large gulp. I was shaking and sweating. Nausea overtook me.

I quickly put down the bottle and glass. I rushed to the bathroom and threw up several times. I flushed the toilet and drug myself over to the sink. I rested my elbows on the edge of the counter and turned on the cold water. I rinsed the vomit out of my mouth and splashed my face. I looked up and saw myself in the mirror. I looked horrible. I felt horrible. This was the worst day of my life. Everything bad that ever happened to me paled in comparison to this. What was I going to do now? I didn't want to hear anymore. I was done. What was I going to do?

A loud crash came from the living room. I flung the bathroom door open and ran down the hall into the living room. Dr. Biterman was standing over my grandfather pointing a gun at him. My grandfather lay on the floor next to the lamp.

"STOP! Don't shoot!"

"It's him, isn't it!? He's in the picture. You recognized him!"

"Please put the gun down. Dr. Biterman, please…"

"He's a murderer! He's a criminal! He deserves to die!"

"He's my grandfather."

"It doesn't matter. He must pay for what he has done."

"What has he done? You don't know!"

"He is SS! He is guilty!"

"Please don't!"

"I have to!"

"NO!"

As he took aim and began to squeeze the trigger, I saw Blondi running from the kitchen. She leapt into the air and sank her teeth into Dr. Biterman's wrist just as he was pulling the trigger.

The shot fired wide and hit the lamp which exploded. Dr. Biterman dropped the gun and fell to the ground. Blondi's teeth remained clinched on his wrist as she thrashed her head back and forth. He screamed in agony. I grabbed Blondi and yelled at her to release. I tried prying her jaws apart with my hands but it was no use. Another shot fired.

Blondi released and ran back into the kitchen. I looked up to see my grandfather standing over Dr. Biterman. A light smoke was coming from the barrel of the .22 he held pointed at Dr. Biterman.

My eyes turned to Dr. Biterman. He lay motionless on his back. His eyes were fixed on the ceiling. His mouth was halfway open. A trickle of blood ran down the side of his head from the bullet hole in the center of his forehead. I couldn't speak. I couldn't move. I was paralyzed.

"Enkel."

I didn't respond.

"Enkel!"

I looked up at him dumbfounded. He held the gun at his side. I didn't know what was going to happen next. Was he going to shoot me now?

"Enkel, you must go."

"Go?"

"Go where?"

"Go home. I will handle this."

"What... what's going to happen now?"

"Go home. I will handle this."

"Please lieber Enkel, go home."

Still holding the gun in his right hand, he pulled me up with his left. He grabbed me by the arm and led me to the front door. He sat the gun down on the hallway credenza. He opened the door and walked me to my truck. He told me to give him my keys. I complied and he started my truck. He had to help me get in the front seat. I turned my head to look at him.

"Go home."

I nodded my head. I don't remember driving home.

Going the Distance

I dragged myself out of bed at 4:00 a.m. I didn't sleep well. Sleeping had been almost impossible since leaving my grandfather's house. I couldn't stop thinking about it. I was a mess. I told Addison it was just nerves.

"Are you OK?"

"Yeah, I'm OK. I'm just nervous about the half Ironman."

I had to do it. I had no choice. Somehow, I had to act normal, as if nothing happened.

I made coffee, and grabbed some breakfast. I loaded my gear and bicycle in my truck. Addison and I drove to Buffalo Springs Lake. We left the house just after 5:00 am. I'm glad we did because when we got there the place was packed. There was a line of cars as far as the eye could see. It was 6:18 am before we got to the parking area. Police were directing traffic.

We unloaded my bike and gear and headed down the hill to the transition area. I had to get my bike on the rack in transition, set out my gear, get my body-marking done, get my wetsuit on and get to the swim start without forgetting anything. Worst of all, I had to do all of this while trying to forget about the nightmare I had been a part of less than 48 hours ago.

It was now 6:48 am. Two minutes to spare. My wave was next. I got a good luck kiss from Addison and rushed over to the swim start. I had my trisuit, wetsuit, watch, timing chip and swim cap on. I licked my goggles, put them on and started stretching.

"Rick!"

I looked up. Ted was walking towards me. I smiled. I didn't know if I was ever going to smile again after being in the middle of a murder scene.

"Ted!"

"Oh, man. Can you believe this? This place is nuts!"

He was right. There were people everywhere. Music and announcements were blaring. People were joking and trying to play off how nervous they were. It was a party-like atmosphere. I was in such a hurry to get ready and so distracted by what else was going on that I hadn't stopped to take it all in.

"I can't believe we're actually doing this!"

"I know!"

A photographer tapped me on the shoulder and motioned for Ted and me to take a picture. We smiled and put our arms around each other.

"Good luck man!"

"Good luck!"

The starting gun fired and I just about jumped out of my skin as the memory of my grandfather holding the smoking gun over Dr. Biterman flashed before my eyes. Instead of running to the water, I stood motionless. I was frozen as if I was back in my grandfather's living room knelt beside Dr. Biterman's body.

Someone shoved me from behind and I almost got trampled as I stumbled into the water. The water wasn't near as cold this time. I started swimming too fast and quickly lost my breath. After the faster swimmers got past me, I was able to calm down and catch my breath. I got a good rhythm going and was swimming steadily. I was even going straight. There's one good thing about being a slow swimmer, you have a lot of people to lead the way. They can't all be off course.

The best part about the swim was that at least for a moment I forgot about the tragedy I was in the middle of. I guess the thought of drowning helps clear your mind. I finished the swim in 43 minutes and 25 seconds. That's a good time for me. I was so glad to get out of the water.

I ran over to my bike and got my wetsuit off a lot quicker this time. I didn't bother to put socks or gloves on either. I put on my helmet, sunglasses and shoes and ran my bike over to the mount line. I hopped on, clipped in my pedals and attacked the hill. I passed three guys going up the hill. This was my part of the race. I was so glad to have my new overpriced tri bike.

Once I got past the hills and out of the canyon my thoughts again returned to what happened. I didn't see my grandfather this morning. He had come to see me do the sprint and gave me hell when Ted beat me. I was hoping he wouldn't show today. I didn't know what I would say or how I would act around him.

I put the hammer down and pedaled like a mad man. I attacked the hills and coming down them I stayed in the aero position. I don't know how I didn't wreck. I was pushing too hard though.

I made it back to the canyon leading into Buffalo Springs Lake and my legs felt weak. I knew I was going to be in trouble when I got to the last hill. I slowed down to conserve energy and downed a packet of energy gel. I eased my cadence. As I got closer to the last hill, I started to sprint.

I hit the hill going as fast as I could and switched gears as I lost momentum. I was in the last gear I had but I couldn't stand up to pedal. My legs were too weak. I sat upright and grabbed the handlebars. I thrust my pedals forward as hard as I could. I was panting and my legs were burning. I was swerving side to side and barely kept moving. As I topped the hill and the road flattened my upper body collapsed on the handlebars as my legs slowly churned.

I got back into the aero position and started switching gears as I sped down the last hill to transition. I slowed down. It was too dangerous to fly through here with all of the people at the bottom. As glad as I was to finish the swim, I was much happier to get off the bike. My ass hurt so badly. I racked my bike and ditched my helmet and shoes. I put on my hat, sunglasses and running shoes. I grabbed my race belt with my bib number on it and clipped it around my waist as I took off running. I tried to run. My legs weren't cooperating.

I made good time on the bike. I finished in less than 3 hours. Now I just had to finish. I had time to walk it if I had to. I had this. What I didn't have was peace of mind. As I exited transition to start the run I saw a police officer standing there. Was he waiting for me? Was I about to be arrested? Just run!

As I expected, the people I passed on the bike started to pass me on the run. I had improved but I still sucked as a runner. I had pushed too hard on the bike and this was going to be a long half marathon. Now I had to run out of the canyon, into and out of another canyon and along a stretch of asphalt with no shade, absolutely none. Then I had to turn around and do it again. It was brutal.

I didn't even bother trying to run up the hills. I could walk faster. I ran as much as I could and tried to only walk through the aid stations but there were times I just had to walk. I had no energy. I downed powerade, drenched myself with water and poured a cup of ice down my tri suit. But all the while, I thought about the mess I had gotten myself into. I saw Ted as I was coming back into the canyon. I was ahead of him.

"Ted!"

"Good job man!"

"Good job!"

I knew I was ahead of him because his bike was still in transition when I was done with the swim and he hadn't passed me on the bike. Victory was mine! I was going to beat him but it didn't matter. I was glad I had done well so far but now I was walking more than running. I managed to finish the race running and finished strong. It took me longer to do the run than the bike, just over 3 hours. Including my transitions times my total race time was 6 hours 39 minutes and 12 seconds. I had done it. I thought of Coke and I wished he could see me now. I wished Dr. Biterman could see me now. I wished he was alive.

"Rick! Rick!"

It was Addison. I started towards her but was stopped by the police officer I saw earlier.

"Hey. Not so fast."

Oh, Shit!

"What?"

"Don't forget your finisher medal."

I can't handle this! I turned around and a volunteer put the medal around my neck and took off my timing chip.

"Great job."

"Thank you, Sir."

I slowly made my way over to Addison.

"I'm so proud of you. You did great."

"Well, I finished anyway."

"Whatever. You did great."

"I beat Ted at least."

"Yes, you did."

We waited for Ted to finish and cheered him across the finish line. Ted and I had done it and we were both exhausted. It was time to go home. We gathered our gear and bikes from transition. I learned the hardest hill was the one you had to walk up after the race to get to your car.

Thank you, Coke. You believed in me when I didn't. You were right. It was worth it.

Paying a Visit

I had plenty of time to think during the triathlon and unfortunately had plenty to think about. We got back to the house and I struggled to get out of the truck. My body had stiffened since we left Buffalo Springs Lake.

"A little stiff, old man?"

"Just a little."

"I'll get your stuff. Go take a shower. You stink."

"I'm sure I do."

I hobbled into the house and made my way to the bathroom. I closed the door and looked at myself in the mirror. I looked like hell. Most of my sweaty body was sunburned. It was very difficult to peel that tri suit off.

After showering and getting dressed, I grabbed a beer and sat on the couch. I twist off the cap and took a long drink. I leaned back and closed my eyes.

"Rick."

"Rick."

"Huh? What?"

I had fallen asleep.

"Rick."

"Yeah, what's up?"

"There are some men here asking for you."

"Police?"

"No."

"Who are they?"

"I don't know. They have strange accents."

"Accents?"

I got up to go to the door forgetting that I had just done a half Ironman. My legs almost gave out on me. I hobbled over to the door and opened it.

There stood two men wearing dark suits and ties. The man in front was small in stature. He wore black horn-rimmed glasses and had a Terry Bradshaw hairline. The remaining hair was almost white. The man behind him looked more like Howie Long. He had short cropped brown hair and his face held no expression. He was almost twice the size of his petite companion. A pin bearing the Star of David was on each of their lapels.

"Can I help you?"

"Are you Rick Rousser?"

"Yes."

"My name is Rafi Amit and this is Mr. Meir Eitman."

"We apologize for bothering you at your home. We are associates of Dr. Eilam Biterman. We had an appointment with him but he did not show. We have been unable to find him. We have made inquiries and understand you are familiar with Dr. Biterman."

"Yes, I am studying under him."

"Ah, then we have come to the right man. May we come in and talk? It will only take a moment."

No!

"Sure. Come on in."

"Please, have a seat. Can I get you gentleman anything?"

"No, thank you Mr. Rousser."

Addison walked into the living room.

"I believe you have met my girlfriend, Addison Haymaker."

Both men stood.

"Nice to meet you, Miss Haymaker."

"My name is Rafi Amit and this is Mr. Meir Eitman."

"Nice to meet ya'll."

"You need anything, honey?"

"No, I'm fine."

"Pardon me, Miss Haymaker. Would you mind if we spoke with Mr. Rousser privately?

"No. Not at all."

"Thank you. You are too kind."

Addison walked into our bedroom and closed the door.

"Please, sit down gentleman."

"Rousser, that's a German name isn't it?"

"Yes, it is."

"Where was your father born?"

"Here."

"Where was your grandfather born?"

"Germany."

"Germany. I see."

"When did your grandfather move to America?"

"After the war."

"World War II?"

"Yes."

"I see."

"Where does your grandfather live?"

"Here."

"I see."

"Mr. Emet? Is it?"

"Amit."

"Mr. Amit. Why are you asking me questions you already know the answers to?"

"Straightforward, Mr. Rousser. I like that."

"Does he speak?"

"Mr. Eitman speaks when he wants to. He is not a social animal like I am."

"Where is your grandfather?"

"I don't know."

"Where is Dr. Biterman?"

"I don't know."

"Do you know who your grandfather is?"

"Do you mean what was his name before he changed it?"

"Yes, that is what I mean."

"No. I don't"

"Do you know what he did during the war?"

"I have an idea."

"You have NO idea!"

I almost jumped out of my skin. Mr. Eitman spoke. I wish he hadn't. He scared the hell out of me. He and Mr. Amit knew it too.

"Mr. Rousser, Mr. Eitman and I are with Mossad. Do you know what Mossad is?"

I hesitated to answer. Mr. Eitman was staring me down.

"Yes. It's the Israeli Secret Intelligence Service."

"Correct. And do you know what we do Mr. Rousser?"

"Yes, I do."

"Ah, now we are getting somewhere. Mr. Rousser, we are very familiar with Dr. Biterman. He is very well respected in the Jewish community. We have relied on him to provide valuable information over the years, valuable information that we have used to find war criminals.

Now, Dr. Biterman has, over the years, been like the boy who cried wolf. There have been numerous instances when he thought he had found someone and it would turn out to be nothing. We would always investigate but find nothing. I mean, really, how many war criminals could there be in Lubbock, Texas?

Dr. Biterman contacted us recently. He was adamant that he found someone of interest. He would not be dissuaded. Again, we agreed to investigate. Like I said, we have a great deal of respect for Dr. Biterman. We think he is right this time."

"Do you know who Dr. Biterman suspects?"

"Yes."

"Do you know what this man did?"

"No."

"That is right. You have no idea."

"This man, your grandfather, was in the SS. He was in command of a killing squad. He most likely could have lived without pursuit if he hadn't taken the initiative. He did much more than just follow orders. Your grandfather is an electrician? Correct?"

"Yes Sir."

"Well, he is being modest. He is actually an electrical engineer. Soon after the invasion of Russia, he offered his services to his superiors. He presented his idea to use electrocution as a means of mass execution. He designed a room that could hold up to fifty people. The floor was made out of a metal plate. It was designed to resemble a shower room. The victims were lured into the rooms believing they were going to take a shower. They were even given bars of soap. Once they were in the room, the door was locked, the drains were closed and the water was turned on. The water would start to flood the room. Once the water level reached ankle height, the floor was electrified. It worked but not well enough for the Nazis.

Zyklon B as used in gas chambers was much more to their liking. It was able to kill more people and do it quicker. Electrocution was not efficient enough to satisfy their needs. They liked the bathhouse idea and kept it as they switched from electric to gas execution. It was almost always 100% effective. On very rare occasions, a half-alive victim would be found under a pile of corpses.

Hinrichtung is the word for electrocution in German. Your grandfather's real name is Heinrich Strom. He earned the moniker "Der Heinrichtungfuhrer". His idea did not provide the Nazis with Die Endlosung, the Final Solution to the "Jewish Question", but it brought him notoriety. Rick, we need to find your grandfather."

"If I knew where he was, I would tell you but I don't."

"That is most unfortunate. Where does your grandfather live?"

You know exactly where he lives.

"A few blocks from here."

"Perhaps you could take us there."

Love to.

"Yes, I can take you there."

"Good."

"Let me grab some shoes."

"Take your time."

I groaned as I got off the couch.

"Congratulations on completing your triathlon. That is quite an accomplishment."

"Thank you."

They knew everything. I was screwed. I walked to our bedroom and opened the door. Addison was sitting on the bed and stood up as I walked in. I could tell she was nervous.

"What do they want?"

"They are looking for my grandfather."

"Why are they looking for your grandfather?"

"They know him from the war."

I grabbed a pair of shoes.

"Where are you going?"

"They want me to take them to my grandfather's house."

"Is everything OK?"

"Yes. Don't worry."

I gave her a kiss and patted her bottom.

"Love you."

"Love you too."

Mr. Amit and Mr. Eitman were both standing in the middle of the living room waiting for me.

"We can take my car."

"OK."

Thank God it was a short drive. Mr. Amit insisted I ride shotgun. Mr. Eitman sat in the back seat directly behind me. That was very unnerving as I knew he could have snapped my neck at any given moment.

Mr. Amit parked in the driveway. We got out of the car and the two gentlemen from Mossad followed me to the front door. I didn't bother ringing the doorbell. I knew he wasn't home.

I had never been in my grandfather's house without him there. He had given me a spare key but I'd never used it. I didn't even know if it worked.

I slid the key in, unlocked the deadbolt and opened the door. The two Mossad agents were standing behind me as Blondi came running to the front door to greet me. She suddenly stopped when she saw the two men following me into her home. She barked ferociously at them. I scolded her and put her in the backyard.

"I'm sorry. She doesn't like strangers. She's really a very sweet dog."

"German Shepherds weren't bred to be sweet dogs."

"Where is your grandfather?"

"I told you. I don't know."

"Mind if we look around?"

"No."

"Perhaps you would be so kind as to give us a tour."

"Of course."

"Your grandfather is a very tidy man."

"Yes, he is."

He was tidy but not this tidy. I had never seen his house so neat. I was terrified that I was going to open the front door and Dr. Biterman's body would be on the living room floor. There was nothing on the floor except for a very clean rug. A recliner was centered in front of the television with a small table next to it minus a lamp. I led them into the kitchen. They noticed the overflowing bowl of dog food and the two large bowls of water that had been left for Blondi.

"Sweet Blondi must have quite an appetite."

It was obvious my grandfather didn't plan on returning anytime soon. I opened the connecting door to the garage and led them in. My grandfather's waxed El Camino was the only thing in it.

"Is this your grandfather's truck?"

"It's not a truck. It's an El...nevermind. Yes, It's his truck."

"Why does it have an "SS" on it?"

Smart ass. He knows that's not what it stands for.

"It stands for Super Sport not Schutzstaffel."

I walked back into the house and led them into his bedroom. He had a queen size bed with a very old comforter on it. There was a dresser with a small mirror. The only picture in the room was a black and white one of his wife, my grandmother, who I never met.

"Is this his wife?"

"Yes, his wife, my grandmother."

"Was she Jewish?"

I turned to look at him. I was surprised by the question.

"Yes, she was."

"Many war criminals married Jewish woman. They thought marrying a Jew would help them from being discovered. Who would ever think someone in the SS would marry a filthy Jew? His dick would probably fall off. And if they were discovered? Surely, they were changed men if they married a Jew. Very clever, don't you think?"

He was trying to get at me and he was.

"Very."

Next was the bathroom and his spare room. Nothing.

"Satisfied, gentlemen?"

"Herr Rousser...excuse me, Mr. Rousser, don't you think this is odd?"

"Herr Amit...excuse me, Mr. Amit, don't I think what is odd?"

"Your grandfather and Dr. Biterman are both missing."

"Yes, it is odd."

I could sense Mr. Eitman standing behind me. Mr. Amit walked up to me, well within my personal space. He took off his glasses revealing his piercing light blue eyes. He studied my face and looked into my eyes. I wasn't sure if he was going to kiss me or kill me. I was scared. My seventh grade black belt was no match for two Mossad agents.

"I don't like uncertainties Mr. Rousser. I am uncertain how much you know. However, I am certain Dr. Biterman discovered who your grandfather really was. I am certain Dr. Biterman did not listen to our instructions and confronted your grandfather. I am certain your grandfather killed Dr. Biterman to protect himself."

He stopped talking and just looked at me. I could feel myself shaking and I started sweating. My heart was pounding and my mouth was bone dry.

"He is dead. Isn't he?"

"Yes."

"Your grandfather killed him?"

"Yes."

"Where do you think your grandfather is?"

"I don't know."

"Where do you think Dr. Biterman's body is?"

"I don't know."

"This is very troubling Mr. Rousser."

"Yes, it is."

"I do appreciate your honesty. It is natural for one to protect one's family, even one with a past... a very certain past indeed."

He put on his glasses and walked around me. Mr. Eitman followed him. They walked out the front door. Mr. Eitman shut the door behind them. My knees gave out and I dropped to the floor. I was physically and emotionally spent.

I managed to compose myself and struggled to stand. I went to the back door and called for Blondi. She was sitting by the gate at the back of the yard. She cautiously approached the house. She turned her head side to side looking for the recent house guests as she entered the kitchen. She followed the trail of their scent around the house. When she was convinced they were gone she came to me. I got down on one knee to pet her. She was shaking. So was I.

"There, there Blondi. It's going to be OK. You're coming home with me."

She followed me to the front door. I opened the door and stepped outside. I placed my hand on the doorknob and looked back inside. There was nothing on the floor except for a very clean rug. A recliner was centered in front of the television with a small table next to it minus a lamp. Blondi stared at me.

"Komm her zu mir Blondi."

She slowly stepped out of the house looking side to side for any unwanted visitors. She stopped in front of me, sat down on the front porch and looked up at me. I closed the front door and locked the deadbolt. I looked down at her.

"Your master is not coming home."

Tel Aviv on TV

Lubbock is a big small town. It had never been more evident since Dr. Biterman and my grandfather went missing. Rumors swirled around town. I put my graduate work on hold. I had no interest in it anymore. Addison suffered as well. She was drug into this. I tried to leave her but she wouldn't let me. She said she loved me and would stay with me no matter what we had to endure. We had done nothing wrong but we suffered. We couldn't go anywhere without people staring at us and whispering. Needless to say, we spent a lot of evenings at home.

It was a month later when I saw it on CNN. I was making breakfast. As I flipped the cooked egg batter over on the bacon and cheese, I heard his name, his real name and the moniker that made him infamous. It was Wolf Blitzer making the announcement. I ran into the living room. The image on the screen was the photograph Dr. Biterman had in his office, the photograph I had shown to my grandfather.

"We have breaking news from Tel Aviv. Sources there tell us that Heinrich Strom, the Nazi war criminal known as the Heinrichtungfuhrer, has been captured. He was discovered in Lubbock, Texas by Mossad, the Jewish Secret Intelligence Service. Strom was a member of the SS who developed a method of mass execution by electrocution that was the precursor to the use of gas chambers."

Strom never made it out of Lubbock. Mossad had found him and flown him to Israel. He was to stand trial for war crimes.

Many years ago, Mossad found Adolf Eichmann, the architect of the Holocaust in Argentina. Eichmann was captured and flown to Israel to stand trial for war crimes. He was found guilty and sentenced to death. He was hung, cremated and his ashes were scattered in the Mediterranean.

My grandfather's fate was sealed. The only thing I didn't know for certain was where his ashes would be scattered.

It had been agonizing to call my father and have to tell him who his father really was. My mother told me he took it very hard. She said he would go to the beach for hours just sitting there staring off into the horizon. When he was home, he would drink too much.

He was devastated by the revelation. Now he would have to endure the trial. It would be a lengthy and internationally publicized criminal trial. Eichmann was captured, put on trial and executed within two years. I was certain Heinrich Strom's fate would be decided just as quickly.

I tried to keep myself busy. Without graduate school and only working twenty hours a week at the pharmacy, I had more time to train. I decided to sign up for Ironman Texas. This was a full Ironman - 2.4 mile swim, 112 mile bike and then you run a marathon. Anything is possible. I learned that life lesson. With all that was going on in my life, I was still able to keep it together and finish the half at Buffalo. I withstood questioning from Mossad. I endured the gossip and sneers of many Lubbockites. I accepted the fact my grandfather was a war criminal and was not long for this world. My only regret was the loss of Dr. Biterman. I replayed the scene in my mind over and over again wondering if there was any way I could have saved him. That will always haunt me.

Ironman Texas was in May in The Woodlands just north of Houston. A few days before the race, I loaded up my truck and headed south. Addison couldn't make the drive with me. She had finals and was going to fly down for the race. I was about halfway there when the humidity began to rise.

My hands were sticking to the steering wheel. It is very humid in South Texas and I knew this was only the beginning. This was one of the many factors that concerned me about the race. I was used to the dryness of West Texas. I made it there in good time, less than eight hours. Texas is a big state.

Unlike Lubbock, The Woodlands is a very wealthy community. Cars such as Bentleys, Lamborghinis, and Aston Martins line the streets in front of the numerous shopping centers, coffee shops, restaurants and bars. There is a lot of oil money and many corporate headquarters are based there as well. It had been a long time since I had been around so many trees. There are no trees in Lubbock. It is flat and you can see for miles around you. The tallest things are the cotton plants. Not so in The Woodlands which you could probably have guessed by the name.

I felt claustrophobic when I moved to Austin for pharmacy school. Claustrophobia was rearing its ugly head again. You couldn't even see stores from the street. There were trees lined along the sidewalks and the only way you knew if something was behind them were by signs at the intersections that were only permitted to be ten feet tall. You couldn't see the signs until you drove up to them. If you weren't in the turn lane, you would miss the turn and have to circle the block. Just trying to get to Target was a nightmare.

The Marriot was the host hotel for the Ironman. It was located directly alongside the canal that would serve as part of the swim course and the sidewalk that would serve as part of the run course. It was also only a block away from the finish line. It was a perfect location. The only problem was the price, $500 a night. My cheap ass wasn't going to fork over that kind of money.

Even if I was willing to throw down that kind of cash, rooms had been reserved months in advance. In fact, most participants reserved their room right after the last race to ensure they got one. This was my first rodeo. Everything was booked. There were almost 2,900 people signed up to do the race. There was an old La Quinta just north of The Woodlands along the interstate. That's where I found a room.

A room at the La Quinta cost $189 a night. That was much more my speed. It was still overpriced for a La Quinta but I didn't have much of a choice. "La Quinta" must be Spanish for "behind Denny's" because they always are. This hotel was no exception.

I checked in and unloaded my bike and gear. After driving around it twice, I had been able to find the local Target. It was north of town as well. Target is not ritzy enough to be in the city limits of The Woodlands. I grabbed some drinks and snacks. The next morning, I drove to the airport and picked up Addison.

"How are your finals going?"

"So far, so good."

She was not excited about the La Quinta. When she found a huge dead cockroach in the bathroom, she was not happy.

"At least it's dead."

"This place is disgusting."

"This is the best I could do. Evidently, this is a very popular race. Everything is booked."

We left her luggage in the room and drove to the Ironman Village so I could check in for the race and pick up my race packet. We had to park blocks away. There were people everywhere. People were riding bikes and running but most were making their way to the village.

There were numerous vendors at the village. Companies were selling goggles, wetsuits, bikes, helmets, running shoes, supplements and every other possible item a triathlete could need. We walked the gauntlet of vendors to the athlete tent. Addison couldn't go in. Only athletes were allowed in the tent. She waited outside for me and I made my way to check-in. I showed a volunteer my USAT (USA Triathlon) card and she gave me my race packet, timing chip and wristband. I was number 655. I was officially a participant.

I was so nervous. I looked around at all of the other competitors in the tent. They were all so fit. There was zero percent body fat on all of them. I had trained hard and was in good shape but looked nothing like these people.

I overheard a couple of people talking about the swim. They were talking about it not being wetsuit legal. There is a rule about wearing a wetsuit. The rule allows participants to wear a wetsuit if the water temperature is 76.1 degrees or less. Ironman Texas had never had a water temperature at or below 76.1 degrees on race day. Shit. I wasn't going to be able to wear a wetsuit.

Wetsuits provide buoyancy making it easier to swim and thus swim faster. I'd never swum in open water in a triathlon without a wetsuit. Would I be able to swim fast enough and avoid the cut-off time of 2 hours and 20 minutes? Granted 2 hours and 20 minutes is a long time but 2.4 miles is a long swim. This wasn't good news.

I made my way to the exit and was given an Ironman Texas backpack full of souvenirs, freebies and coupons from the vendors. It cost almost $700 to sign up for the Ironman so I figured I had actually paid for the backpack and souvenirs. I told Addison about the water temperature and wetsuit restriction. My only option was to get a speed suit.

A speed suit is a piss poor substitute for a wetsuit. It's basically a swimsuit the same size as a tri suit. It's very lightweight, thin and slick. It provides some hydrodynamic advantage. I had never worn one or even owned one so we went shopping.

We found a vendor selling them. The only one left in my size was the most expensive, of course. It was the top of the line speed suit. It cost $379.99. I didn't care. I would have bought it even if cheaper ones were available. I wasn't going to skimp on something that might determine if I finish the swim in time. Addison was shocked by the prices of everything.

"I know. I could have picked a less expensive hobby."

We found a Mexican restaurant and had lunch. Addison wanted to go do her kind of shopping so we walked over to Market Street, the high-end outdoor shopping area. There was a central park with freshly mowed grass. At one end of the park was a large, ornate covered gazebo used for plays, shows and concerts. Park benches, statues of children playing and fountains lined the border of the park. At the other end of the park was a restaurant with a large outdoor patio facing the Gazebo across the way. Shops surrounded the park. At each overpriced store entrance, umbrellas were available for the well-to-do patrons. Intermittent showers were common in this humid environment. Perish the thought that they might get wet going from store to store spending absurd amounts of money. We were window-shopping.

We happened upon a Lululemon store that had the shape of Texas outlined with the names of the participants in the Ironman on a large window next to the front door. I found my name and Addison took a picture of me pointing at it. It was really cool and added to the excitement of the event. We drove back to the hotel, made love and took a nap. We got ready for the athlete dinner being held that evening at the Marriot.

The dinner was a huge event. It was set up as a self-serve buffet line with chicken, steak, vegetables, mashed potatoes, rolls and an assortment of desserts. The majority of the participants had been on a strict diet leading up to the race but now they were cutting lose and enjoying themselves.

We sat down at one of the many large tables in the hall in front of a large stage. There were two large screens, one on each side of the stage. We began to eat and visited with the others at our table. It was interesting to hear how other people had made their way to this point in their lives. The dinner was hosted by Mike Reilly, "The Voice of Ironman." He was the one who would call out your name at the finish line and declare "You are an Ironman!" That is what every would-be Ironman wanted to hear.

Mike began by thanking the race sponsors. The sponsors presented enormous cardboard checks to charities. Chris McDonald, an Ironman Champion known as "Big Sexy", was the keynote speaker. He started doing triathlons because he was overweight and out of shape. Although he was never much of an athlete, he kept training and doing more triathlons. He got good at them, very good. He qualified for the world championship in Kona and won. His was a great story.

After Big Sexy's speech, Mike Reilly took over again. He spouted off the number of first time Ironman participants and those who were repeat Ironman Texas participants. There were triathletes from every state and eighteen countries. Then he introduced some particular triathletes. One was a man who had lost over 200 pounds! He had done Ironman Texas last year and missed the midnight cutoff by thirty-five seconds. He vowed to make it this year. He received more applause than anyone else and deservedly so.

The youngest participants were a couple of 18-year-olds. Eighteen is the youngest age allowed to participate. There were two slots to Kona for their age group. All they had to do to secure a slot to Kona was to finish.

The majority of the participants were middle-aged. Apparently, this was a popular mid-life crisis event. The oldest participant was eighty-one. If he finished he was going to Kona as well. We finished dinner, went back to the hotel and crashed.

The next morning, I got my bike and gear bags ready. Tomorrow was the big day and all of the age-group athletes had to leave their bikes and gear bags at transition today. I racked my bike among the sea of other bicycles. I looked around at the surrounding area trying to memorize by bike's location. They were grouped in order by number but finding your bike after the swim still wasn't easy, especially when there were almost 3,000 of them.

We had lunch at Pallotta's. It's an Italian restaurant in The Woodlands that was recommended by the owner of Velocity Bike Shop. Velocity is the best bike shop in Lubbock and the owner recommended the restaurant when I took my bike in to get it tuned up before the race. I told him I wanted to make sure it was ready for Ironman Texas. I was taking no chances.

A breakdown on the bike could cost me valuable time. He told me his best friend owned the restaurant and we should eat there. It was a good recommendation. Although I only got a simple dish of spaghetti and meatballs, it was absolutely delicious.

We saw the owner going around the restaurant greeting people and making sure everything was prepared to their liking. He looked like Dom Deluise. He looked like what you would expect an Italian Chef to look like, large and round. He made his way to our table, introduced himself and asked how everything was. Addison and I both agreed our meals were excellent and I told him I knew his best friend who recommended his restaurant to us. He smiled and slapped me on the back almost knocking me out of my chair.

"That's great. So, you guys are from Lubbock?"

"That's right."

"What brings you to The Woodlands? The cool weather?"

He laughed.

"We're here for the Ironman."

"Oh, wow. Well, I can see you're carb loading. I'm glad I could help. Nice to meet you two and best of luck in your race."

"Nice to meet you as well. Thank you."

After lunch we went looking for a steak place. I figured this might be my last chance to have a good steak if I drown on the swim. I might as well go out in style. We found a Fleming's steak house that was right down the street from the Marriot and made a reservation for dinner.

We went to the local mall and did more shopping. Man, Addison likes to shop. It wears me out. We headed back the hotel, made love and took a nap. We got ready for my last meal and headed to Fleming's. The steak was great. The price was not. After dinner, we went to The Cheesecake Factory for dessert. I got a slice of the red velvet cake. I ate the whole thing and almost made myself sick. Then it was back to the hotel. I checked and rechecked and rechecked my gear for tomorrow. I was stressing out.

"Relax. You'll do fine."

"I know."

I didn't know. I had trained and tried to prepare myself as much as possible. I felt like I didn't know what I was doing and had bitten off more than I could chew.

"Come to bed."

"All right."

"Are you going to snuggle me tonight?"

"Of course, I always snuggle you."

"No you don't."

I couldn't go to sleep. We had to get up at 4:00 am. Transition opened at 5:00 am and I wanted to eat breakfast and check my bike's tire pressure before we headed over to the swim start. I watched TV for a while and finally turned it off. I fell asleep just after midnight. We got up at 4:00am and got ready to go.

"You got everything?"

"I think so."

"Don't forget your speed suit."

Damn it. I almost forgot it. I was nervous and couldn't think straight.

There was no parking near the swim start. Everyone had to walk. There was a juggernaut of people headed that way. The swim was in Lake Woodlands, not a very original name I know. It is a man-made lake that leads into the canal in front of the Marriot. The swim would be in a large rectangular shape before taking a right turn into the canal. It was chaos when we got there.

There were lines of people waiting to use the port-o-potties. A triathlon is the one place where you will see more men waiting in line to use the toilet than women. I found a volunteer with a black marker and got my numbers written on my upper arms and my age written on my left calf. I had my tri suit on under the shirt and shorts I was wearing. I took my shirt and shorts off and put on my speed suit. There were 45 minutes before the race would start. I got in line to use a port-o-potty. I didn't need to use one but I figured by the time I got to the front of the line I would. After waiting in line forever, I did need to do my business.

I got my swim cap and goggles from Addison just minutes before the professional triathletes were to start. The age-groupers would start afterwards. She told me her mom, Tina, had called to wish me good luck. My parents had called to do the same the evening before. I kissed Addison and she wished me good luck. I headed to the swim start.

The male professionals started first. The female professionals started 10 minutes after them. It was almost 7:00 am, time for everyone else to start. We were herded into the lake like cattle. I quickly moved to the back of the pack with the buoys lined up on my left.

I was treading water and wishing that I had my wetsuit on. The water wasn't cold but I sure missed the buoyancy. I was taking deep breaths and trying to calm myself. The starting gun fired and it was mass hysteria.

I started swimming and quickly realized I was pushing too hard again. I lost my breath and was struggling so I slowed down and got my breathing under control. Faster swimmers were swimming around and over me. Before getting to the first turn buoy, I was able to draft off other swimmers. That was a first for me and it does make a difference. I was moving steadily and glanced at my watch as I made the first turn. It read 56:13. I was going too slow!

My breathing was relaxed and I wasn't too tired. It was time to pick up the pace or I wasn't going to make it in time. I put my head down, extended my reach, increased the force at the end of my stroke and started kicking harder. I only glanced up a few times to make sure I was going straight. I didn't look at my watch again until I got to the turn that led to the canal. It read 2:01:03. I had less than 19 minutes to make it.

I should be OK. I didn't like it being over two hours already though. I was swimming hard and out of breath. My lungs were burning and I had to pause longer when I rotated to take deeper breaths. People lined the canal and were cheering swimmers on. I could see people and hear them yelling as my head turned side to side. I wondered if I would see Addison cheering me on.

The water was shallow in the canal. Some people stopped to stand and rest. I wasn't about to. I was going to make it out of that canal on time no matter what. The canal wasn't a straight shot. It snaked along the buildings and I couldn't see the last buoy. I wasn't sure how far I was from the finish. Every time I came around a corner I looked for but couldn't see the last buoy. I looked at my watch. It read 2:10:23. I swam around the next corner and there it was - the final buoy. Thank God! The longest part of the swim was around that last buoy. I made the turn and sprinted for the stairs leading out of the canal. I got close enough to stand on the first row of stairs. A volunteer grabbed my hand and steadied me as I climbed out of the canal.

"Good job."

Not really.

"Thank you."

I could barely say anything because I was breathing so hard. I had made it out of the water in 2:11:12. I had less than nine minutes left to make it. That was a lot closer than I expected. I was disappointed with my performance but very glad I made it out in time. Addison was on the other side of the fence cheering for me. I waved at her as I ran towards the men's transition tent.

It wasn't too hard to spot my gear bag. They were in numerical order just as the bikes were and there weren't many bags left. Almost everyone was ahead of me. I grabbed my bag and ran inside the changing tent. I emptied my bag on the ground. I peeled off my speed suit and threw it, my goggles and swim cap into the gear bag. I put on my helmet and sunglasses and picked up my bike shoes.

I ran out of the tent to the bike racks. I ran down the center aisle looking for the surrounding area I tried to memorize earlier. One of the volunteers called out my number to another volunteer in the middle of the bikes. She directed me to my bike.

I put on my shoes and un-racked my bike. I ran with my bike to the mount line and jumped on it.

I put the hammer down! I was pumped and wanted to make up time. For the first 30 miles, I averaged almost 22 miles per hour. It was a beautiful ride through the woods especially going through Sam Houston State Park. For the next 30 miles I averaged 17 miles an hour. The adrenaline was running out and my legs were getting tired. My boney butt hurt so bad. That pain was almost worse than my aching legs.

All I wanted to do was get off that bike. I stopped at the next aid station. I realized I hadn't needed to pee since I started the race. It was 91 degrees with 75% humidity putting the heat index at 100 degrees. I was getting dehydrated. I had to push the fluids.

I downed a bottle of water and then a bottle of Powerade. There were kiddy pools filled with ice water positioned under shade tents. Cyclists were laying in them trying to cool down. I noticed more and more people stopping on the side of the road. There were twice as many people at this aid station than I had seen at any other all day. There was a woman sitting in the shade crying. I went to check on her and I did my best to console her.

"You're over halfway through the bike. You can do this. You've got plenty of time to finish. Take your time and push the fluids and you'll be fine."

She stopped crying.

"OK but I'm not running! I'm going to walk the damn run."

There was a guy from Seattle who said this was his fifth and last Ironman. He swore to never do this again. He looked exhausted and miserable. One advantage I did have was heat tolerance. It's a necessity in West Texas. I wasn't used to the humidity but I was used to 100 degree days. I loaded up on nutrition, took a salt tablet and got back on the bike.

I knew I had to keep going. I made it about 15 more miles before stopping and getting off my bike at the intersection of a dirt road. I walked my bike to the shade provided by the tall trees. There were trees everywhere except next to the highway. There was a fifteen to twenty foot gap of land between the highway and the trees on each side of the road. There was plenty of shade but it never reached the highway. It was full sun all the way.

I leaned my bike against a tree and took all of the nutrition I had out of my fuel belt. I sat down and leaned back against a tree. I ate a protein bar, granola bar, bagful of chews, and three gus. I ate everything I had. I took my shoes off and massaged my feet. I put my shoes back on, closed my eyes and leaned back against the tree. I sat there for a couple of minutes. I looked at my tri seat and wished I had some well-padded bicycle shorts on. I stood up and walked my bike back to the shoulder of the road. I looked back to make sure no one was coming and I got back on the bike. I stopped at the next aid station and got in the shade again. The disheartened Ironman from Seattle stopped there as well. He was still bitching.

OK, enough. I'm not stopping again. I'm ready to get off this bike and be done. I hopped by sore ass back on the bike and hit the road again. I finally hit 100 miles. The end was so close. There were small rolling hills the whole way back into The Woodlands but it felt like I was climbing in and out of the canyons at Buffalo. I was exhausted.

Addison saw me make it back to transition. She also saw me wobbling on my bike and turn the wrong direction. I was completely out of it. I began to wonder if I had a heat stroke. I figured if I had enough sense to wonder if I had one that meant I didn't. A volunteer got me turned in the right direction and I made it to the dismount line. Finally, I was done with the bike.

Another volunteer took my bike and racked it for me. Addison was along the fence cheering me on. I waved and tried to smile at her. I grabbed my run gear bag and went into the transition tent. I collapsed into a chair. The tent was a disaster. The grass had been trampled into mud. There was trash everywhere. I looked around and everyone had the thousand yard stare, including me. I took my shoes off first, then my helmet. It felt so good. I put on my race belt, running shoes and hat. A volunteer handed me a cup of ice water and helped me put my bike gear in my empty race bag. I finally had to pee. That was a good sign. I hit the port-o-potty.

I came back in the tent and drank some more ice water and put on sunscreen. It was time for the run. I had no idea it took me over 24 minutes to complete the second transition. I walked out of the tent and saw volunteers putting sunscreen on athletes. I walked over and gladly accepted the offer of sunscreen. I was now fully coated. It was too little too late though. I got baked on the bike. I could at least keep from burning anymore. It was also an excuse to delay the inevitable run. After I was coated in sunscreen, I took off. Well, sort of.

My legs would not cooperate. I could barely run. I couldn't lift my knees or kick my feet up to my butt. I "ran" along the sidewalk just feet away from the canal.

It was a party atmosphere. People were drinking and dancing. Music was blaring. Women were dancing in bikinis and groping guys as they ran by. Guys were wearing speedos and drumming on trash cans. It was hysterical. Messages of encouragement were everywhere along the run course. There were pictures and posters along the path. There were messages written in chalk on the sidewalk and streets. I saw where Addison had written "I'm so proud of and love you. Go #665".

I managed to pathetically run along the canal but started walking as soon as I was away from the crowd. Pride and shame kept me running up to that point. I wasn't the only one. There were a lot of people walking. The day had taken it's toll on a lot of people. There were still many miles to go.

How the hell did Coke ever do this? And win? I began to think of Addison, Coke, my parents, my brother, Ted, my grandfather and Dr. Biterman. My failed marriage was a distant memory and didn't even bother me anymore. All the pain and anguish was now pointless. Or, was it actually necessary to get to this point of acceptance and much welcomed apathy? Now I was trying to do something positive for Addison, my family, my friends and myself. I wasn't doing it very well but I was doing an Ironman.

The run course was three loops. It went along the canal in front of the Marriot, out to Lake Woodlands and through the neighborhoods surrounding the lake before returning to downtown. I walked most of the first loop. I just couldn't run. People walking were passing me as I was walking. I even walked slow!

I started the second loop and ran the gauntlet along the canal. As the run course turned away from the canal, I started to walk again. I looked at my watch and realized I was running out of time! If I continued to walk, I wouldn't make the midnight cut off. I had to run the rest of the race to finish in time. At the next aid station I downed a cup of Coke, half a banana, an orange slice and some pretzels.

As I exited the aid station, I began to run, if you could call it that. There were people walking faster than I was running. I had to keep moving though. I couldn't walk fast enough to finish before midnight. I had to run and I did. I was running pathetically slow but I kept running. It was more of a forward stumble than a run. My feet were barely coming off the pavement. The sun had gone down and the partying crowd had dwindled significantly. The only raucous crowd left was at the finish line. I could hear them as I started my last loop.

There weren't many of us left on the run course. It was nearing midnight and some were not going to make it. I was growing more determined. I was not going to go through all I endured today and not finish in time. There was no way I wasn't going to make it. Spectators and volunteers kept up the encouragement. My right hip began to hurt more than anything else. It was my sciatic nerve. The pain started shooting down the side of my leg to my knee. I was heel striking. I lifted my head and stuck out my chest to get my body upright. I forced my heels up and started landing more on the balls of my feet. The pain, at least that pain, subsided. I couldn't remember ever being this tired and hurting this much. I just wanted to stop. The swim was hard. The bike was horrible. This was brutal.

I stopped getting water and snacks at the aid stations. I was tired of fueling myself. I felt like a car that was about to throw a rod. I figured if I did make it to the finish line, I was going to collapse. As I got back to the canal, people were heading home. I saw people wearing their finisher medals. I was going to get one of those! I was hell bent now. I could barely hear the crowd at the finish line. I had less than an hour left to finish the race.

I tried to pick up the pace but it wasn't happening. The volunteers were starting to pack up but were still encouraging racers. The closer it got to midnight the more enthusiastic the spectators and volunteers got. The clock was ticking and some of us were not going to make it. I kept calculating my pace in my head and I had enough time to make it, at least I thought I did. I was exhausted and couldn't think straight. I made the last turn along the canal and was finally headed to the finish line. That was the longest run of my life.

As I got closer, more and more people were lined along the course. Music was blaring and people were cheering. They were reaching across the fence with their hands out for me to slap them. I didn't have the energy but I stuck my hands out and let theirs' slap against mine as I passed them. I saw the finish line and thought I had made it but as I got closer I saw the course took a right turn. The course had a long skinny horseshoe at the end. The finish line was just across from me but I still had to run down and back to finish. There were people everywhere. It was so loud. I didn't have the strength to smile but I was. I made the final turn and it was a straight shot to the finish. I could see Mike Reilly.

I had heard him yelling, "You are an Ironman", when I was running along the canal. Now, I was going to hear it for myself. I began to sprint. When I was a boy my father taught me to always leave enough in the tank to sprint at the end. It may be what you need to win. Obviously, I wasn't going to win today but I was going to finish strong.

"Rick Rousser from Lubbock, Texas. Rick, you… are… an Ironman!"

I finished the race with less than 15 minutes remaining. My time was 16:46:27. A volunteer helped me to a first aid tent but I told him I was fine. He took the timing chip off my ankle. I turned around to find the exit and looked for Addison. A volunteer came up to me and put the medal around my neck. I forgot all about the finisher medal. Another volunteer asked me if I was OK. I must have really looked bad.

I heard her call my name. I turned and saw her directly across from me on the other side of the fence. I slipped between two sections of the fence and she hugged me tightly.

"I'm so proud of you! I was scared you weren't going to make it in time."

"Me too. This is the dumbest thing I've ever done. I need to sit down."

She helped me to the curb and we sat. She handed me a bottle of water and I took small sips. She tried talking to me but I was too tired to have a conversation. It felt like we had just sat there for a couple of minutes when she said we needed to get going so I could get cleaned up and get some sleep. She told me we had been sitting there over 20 minutes. I was a mess. It was past midnight and I had to drive her to the airport in the morning so she could get back to Lubbock for her last final on Monday.

"Yeah, let's get going."

"You know…a grandmother with an artificial leg beat you."

I laughed.

"Is that so?"

She had to help me up off the curb. She already picked up my bike and gear so all we had to do was get to the truck and then drive to the motel. It was a slow walk to the truck. My body temperature began to drop and I got very cold.

When we got back to the motel I took a very hot bath. When I got out I put on pants, socks and all the shirts I had and got in bed. I pulled the sheet tight to my chin. I was shivering.

"Are you cold?"

"I'm freezing."

I now understood why so many of the triathletes at the finish line had space blankets around them. I still wasn't warm when I fell asleep. Addison gently woke me in the morning. She let me sleep as long as possible but now she had to get to the airport.

"Sorry, babe. Time to go."

"OK."

I rolled over on my side and let my feet fall to the floor. She helped me sit up and laughed.

"Sore?"

"Just a little."

I made it out of bed and stripped down to one shirt. She had everything packed and ready. When we got to the elevator there was an out of order sign taped to it. Lucky me, I got a room on the third floor. Addison took the bike. It wasn't heavy just cumbersome. I drug the luggage down the stairs. My legs were not happy with me. That was a long walk downstairs.

I got Addison to the airport in time. She again told me how proud she was of me. She also again pointed out the fact that a one-legged grandmother beat me.

"Thanks. I almost forgot."

"Did you notice what song was playing when you crossed the finish line?"

"I have no idea."

"I'm Sexy and I Know It."

"That's funny."

Back to Bali

I made it home, barely. I had to stop and take a nap a couple of times. Massive amounts of coffee didn't faze me. I had the windows rolled down, the music blaring and I was slapping myself the whole way home.

"I was worried about you. I felt so bad that you had to drive yourself home."

"It's OK. You had to get back for your final."

"I'm glad to be home. Will you give me a hand with my stuff?"

"Sure."

"Are you looking forward to our trip?"

"Of course, I can't wait to finally see Bali. You won't shut up about it."

"You're going to love it. Do you still have some cyclobenzaprine?"

"Yes."

"Good. I need some."

"I bet you do."

She had just finished her spring semester and I was ready to get away for a while. Heinrich Strom was still front-page news. I tried not to think about him while we were in The Woodlands and as I was abusing myself in the Ironman. Now I was home and back to reality. It would still be some time before he went to trial so the media had plenty to talk about.

If only a celebrity would do something stupid to take the attention away from him. Surely there was something more important in the world to talk about than an old man on trial for a crime committed so many years ago. I knew it was necessary though. Crimes of this nature have no statute of limitations nor should they.

The most important life lesson that I learned from Dr. Biterman is that we have a duty to remember those tragic moments in history that could have been prevented by human intervention. "History may try to repeat itself but that doesn't mean we have to allow it to do so." This was one of his favorite sayings.

Addison and I were going to drive to San Diego and then fly to Bali. I wanted to stop and see my parents. I was looking forward to spending a few days with them. I hadn't been to San Diego since the spring break road trip of my senior year in high school. It seemed like yesterday but it also seemed like a century ago. My life had taken so many twists and turns since then.

"When do you want to leave?"

"Tomorrow."

"Tomorrow? You just got home. Do you feel up to it? I'll have to drive the whole way there. You're still exhausted."

"I'll be all right."

"Whatever."

She was not excited and I probably wasn't going to be much help driving. It was out of the way but I wanted to go to Santa Fe first.

"Santa Fe? Is that along the way?"

"No. I like Santa Fe. I just want to go there."

"Oh, brother. Now I have to drive us to Santa Fe."

"Are you sure Ted is capable of taking care of Bailey? I know he's capable of killing animals and putting them on his walls but how is he at keeping one alive?"

"Bailey will be fine."

"What about Blondi?"

"She's coming with us."

"To Bali?"

"No. My parents are adopting her."

"Really?"

"Yes. Their dog just died. They're real dog lovers and didn't hesitate when I asked them if they wanted her. They haven't seen Blondi since she was a puppy."

"Great. Now I have to drive you and Blondi to Santa Fe."

We hit the road the next day after her last final. Addison stopped in Fort Sumner, New Mexico to get gas.

"Why are there so many signs about Billy The Kid here?"

"This is where he was killed. We should go see his grave."

"Why?"

"Because we're here. We just passed it on the way into town. We won't go to the museum. It's a tourist trap and there is hardly anything in there relating to Billy The Kid."

So, we went to the gravesite. She was not impressed but, of course, I always find history interesting. The Old West was a fascinating time. Only World War II has more books written about it. Blondi was not impressed either.

"Can we go now?"

"Yes. I'll drive."

"Can you stay awake?"

"Yes. I like this drive."

I wasn't artsy fartsy as my Dad calls people from Santa Fe but there is a certain something about it. There are artists, authors, composers, nature enthusiasts, homeless and just plain weirdos living there in the high desert. Summer temperatures are comfortable and the skiing is good in the winter.

The historic town square is the heart of the city. Native Americans line the square hawking their turquoise jewelry to tourists. Almost all of the buildings are adobe. Restaurants, cafes, bars, coffee shops, clothing stores, jewelry stores and art sellers line the streets that branch away from the square. Just off the square is San Miguel Chapel. It's the oldest church in the United States. It was built in 1610. It is not a museum though. It's still a functioning church.

My favorite painting is one of Santa Fe. It's a view from the square looking up the street towards San Miguel Chapel. It's winter and the street, sidewalks, cars and church are all topped with snow. The Sangre de Cristo Mountains loom in the background. It's an acrylic on canvas painting by Paul Milosevich, a former art professor from Texas Tech.

We stayed long enough to walk around a bit and grab a bite to eat. Addison wasn't very impressed but I appreciated being there again. It brought back memories of stopping there on the way to and from our backpacking trips in Colorado.

We didn't see much else besides the Grand Canyon on our way to San Diego. Addison was impressed by that. It's hard not to be. It's pretty amazing. Blondi was not impressed.

We made it to San Diego in three days. I was surprised when my father answered the door and gave me a hug. He was not the affectionate type. My mother hugged me as well but that was no surprise. I introduced Addison. My father shook her hand and my mother gave her a bear hug. My mother grew teary eyed.

"Addison, we are so glad to finally meet you."

"Oh, and look at you Blondi! You've grown so much!"

Blondi couldn't wave her tail fast enough.

We visited all afternoon. My father had asked me to bring my finisher medal from Ironman Texas. I pulled it out of my bag and handed it to him. My mother quickly took it away from him to look at it.

"We're so proud of you son."

"There's not much to be proud of. I didn't win. I just finished in time."

"He got beat by a one-legged grandmother."

They got a good laugh out of that.

My parents showed us around San Diego. We went to Balboa Park and toured the Midway. I remembered seeing a company providing hang gliding lessons from the top of the tallest cliffs above Black's Beach. I saw it years ago when Robby and I stopped here on our way to Cabo. It was the Torrey Pines Gliderport.

I had to try hang gliding before we left for Bali. My father and Addison were OK with it but my mother was a nervous wreck. I got paired with a veteran hang glider and was strapped in the hang glider with him. We picked up the hang glider and ran off the edge of the cliff. He handled the glider effortlessly. He even let me steer a little. We were soaring above million dollar homes at the cliff's edge. I could barely make out the nude sunbathers below us on Black's Beach. I looked out over the Pacific and could see a tanker off in the distance. I could see La Jolla just south of us. We glided slowly back and forth into the wind to gain altitude as we made our way back to the gliderport. It was a soft landing. It was awesome. I had done something I wasn't able to do years ago. Mission accomplished. I could mark that one off the bucket list.

We spent our last day relaxing on the beach. Blondi had never seen sand before and loved running in it. She ran and jumped into the surf and fetched anything we threw. She would be happy here and I could tell my parents were thrilled to have her.

The next day we were going to catch the first of many flights to Bali. There was no direct flight to Diver Dan's Scuba Tours. I was packing when my Dad knocked on the door frame. I looked up to see him standing in the door way.

"Hey."

"Want to go for a walk?"

"Sure."

I knew he wanted to talk. It was late in the evening but early enough that the Sun hadn't dipped into the Pacific yet. We walked on the sidewalk in front of the tightly grouped homes along their street. We walked for a couple of blocks before he said anything.

"Let's go sit in the park."

"OK."

I was nervous. I hadn't felt this nervous since I was sandwiched between Mr. Amit and Mr. Eitman. We sat down on a park bench. There was the acceptable distance between us expected for two men sitting on the same piece of furniture.

"Seen the news lately?"

"Yeah."

"I still can't believe it. I'm glad your grandmother isn't alive. Hell, this would have killed her."

"I'm sorry Dad."

"I'm sorry for you Rick. I wish I had been the one mixed up in all of this. You shouldn't have had to deal with it."

"It's OK Dad. I made it through."

"How are you doing?"

"Better. It's been hard to deal with. It's not something one could ever imagine happening to them. What of your professor, Dr. Biterman? Did they ever find him?"

He had been watching the news. He knew about Dr. Biterman's disappearance.

"No. He's dead. I'm sure of it."

And I was.

He nodded his head.

"It's good to see you. It's been too long."

"Yes, it has. I've enjoyed seeing you and Mom. What do you think of Addison?"

"I think you've got a winner there. Let's head home before it gets dark."

As we left the park my father looked down a side street. He stopped me.

"Come here."

I walked over to him. The light from the sunset illuminated his face. As I got closer, I could see the reflection of the sunset in his eyes. I turned and saw the Sun sinking into the Pacific. It was a beautiful sight. We stood there for a meaningful moment.

"OK. Enough of this crap. Let's go home."

He wasn't over the revelation that his father may not be now but was most certainly a monster at one time. It would probably haunt him the rest of his life but, good or evil, Strom was still his father.

I had my childhood memories and the recent memories of my interviews with him. Those interviews were all lies. I felt guilty about Dr.Biterman's death and wished he shot my grandfather when he had the chance. He didn't deserve to die, Strom did.

It was tragic to think he had survived the Holocaust only to be killed by one of it's henchmen years later. I couldn't help but think if only I hadn't gone back to school, if only I hadn't seen that picture, if only I hadn't learned the truth. If only...I suddenly remembered what Addison asked me, "Why is a pharmacist studying history?" That was a very good question. Ignorance is bliss.

We left Addison's car at my parent's house and they gave us a ride to the airport. My father hugged me for the second time in my life as we said our goodbyes. My mother was crying as she hugged us.

"Ya'll be careful."

"We will."

We were off. There wasn't a fast way to get to Bali. Our first flight was to Tokyo, 12 hours and 14 minutes. Our next flight was to Densapar, 7 hours and 35 minutes. Our last flight was to Mataram, a mere 45 minutes. We were exhausted and felt like hell.

I wanted to rent a car and hit the road as soon as we landed on Lombok. Addison was having none of it though. She wanted to get a room and sleep. I didn't argue. We needed it. I could see Coke tomorrow.

We had purchased one way tickets because I wanted us to stay as long as we wanted to. I knew Coke would give us a place to stay. Addison had never been scuba diving and I wanted her to learn. I talked her out of getting lessons before we came because I wanted Coke to teach her and I promised we would stay until she was sick of scuba diving. We arrived in Mataram on the last flight. We got a room and slept until 4 o'clock the next day. We checked out and paid for two nights. We got directions to the closest car rental and barely got one before they closed. We found a street vendor and got one of the Bali burritos Addison listened to me rave about. They were good but not as good as the one I remembered getting here the first time I arrived in Mataram. At that moment, it was the best thing I had ever tasted. Of course, I was suffering from a hangover due to a three day drunk.

I realized how stupid I was to have made such a mess of myself over a worthless woman. My drinking like that was slow suicide. I didn't want to live but I wasn't going to put a bullet through my head. I didn't realize it or at least didn't want to admit it but I had chosen to end it all at the bottom of a bottle. Coke snapped me out of it. He picked me up and dusted me off. He had a tragic and traumatic event in his life that he was trying to live with. He took care of me and forced me to grow up and be a man. I couldn't wait to see him. I hadn't known him for very long but he was one of the most important people in the world to me.

The Sun was setting as we began the drive to Kuta. It soon disappeared into the ocean and the night turned pitch-black. I was speeding along the winding road to Kuta. I was impatient and wanted to get there as soon as possible. I was also making Addison nervous. She yelled at me to slow down. That was the first time she ever yelled at me and I knew she meant business. I slowed down.

It was late when we pulled into town. There were only a handful of lights on and the streets were empty. The few places to stay had no vacancies. There were a lot of surfers in town. Addison didn't want to sleep on the beach so we slept in the car. We woke up with the sunrise. It had been a long journey from Lubbock to Lombok. We were both so relieved we finally made it here and were looking forward to some rest and relaxation.

We drove to the dive shop. My Ironman finisher medal was in my pocket and I was dying to show it to Coke. The painted red letters reading "Diver Dan's" may have faded a bit but the shop looked just as I remembered it. Addison followed me to the front door. I was hoping Coke just made a fresh pot of coffee and hadn't taken a group of tourists on an early morning dive but it didn't look like he was there.

The front of the dive shop had a large walk up counter with a Dutch door in the middle. Horizontal wooden panels were attached to the ceiling by hinges. He would open them to the outside and prop them up to provide shade for would-be customers. He rarely had them closed. I knocked on one of the panels hoping he was inside and just hadn't opened for business yet.

There was no response so I turned the knob on the half door below the middle panel. It was unlocked. I opened the door and ducked inside.

"Are you sure you should be going in there?"

"Yes, Coke won't mind."

I flipped open the center panel and propped it up. Addison stood by the door as I looked around. It didn't look like Coke had been there yet.

"Well, let's go see if he's home. He's usually here by now."

I lowered the panel and closed the half door behind me. We made our way to his house, well home anyway. I had never been in his home but I knew where he lived.

It was a bamboo structure with a thatched roof. It looked like a shack from the outside but it was well constructed. Coke built it himself. We stepped onto his front porch. It had a rocking chair on it. I knocked on the door. No answer. I knocked again. There was still no answer. I turned the knob to see if it was unlocked. It was. I opened the door and stepped inside.

"Are you just going to walk into every place in this town like you own it?"

"It's Coke. He won't mind."

Addison followed me. We walked into a small living room. There was a TV but I doubt there was much to watch. Kuta didn't have a cable company. People came here to get off the grid not to keep up with the outside world.

In front of the television was an uncomfortable looking bamboo couch with gaudy tropical flower cushions on it. There was a small coffee table between the TV and couch. I could see Coke kicking back on the couch with his feet propped up on the coffee table.

There were pictures hanging on the wall behind the couch. There was a picture of him finishing an Ironman. I walked over to it and realized that it was a picture of him winning an Ironman. It was him winning Kona! Next to the picture was another frame. It was his medal. "Ironman World Champion" was written across a large medal in the shape of the Big Island.

"Wow."

"What?"

"Coke told me he was an Ironman. I believed him. I knew he was telling me the truth but to see him coming across the finish line and his medal is amazing."

I stood there shaking my head and smiling.

"Wow."

Next to his medal was a picture of him with a beautiful woman and a cute little girl. The woman could have been a model. She had dark hair and striking light blue eyes. The little girl had bleach blonde hair like Coke. Her hair was in pigtails and she was missing a front tooth.

"Is that his wife and daughter?"

"Must be."

"You never met them?"

"No."

"They died in a car accident."

I walked down the hall and glanced in the kitchen and bedroom. No one was there.

"Where is he? Let's go check at his favorite breakfast spot. Bumbu's is the best place for breakfast. Well, the only place really."

It would be good to see Bumbu again. He was the most colorful character in town. I could smell the coffee and his cooking before we turned the corner. They hadn't been open long. We walked in and sat down at a table.

There wasn't much to Bumbu's. It had a few tables to serve patrons and a bar that was a hang out for the locals. It was usually open sunup to sundown. I saw a young lady behind the bar cleaning glasses. She waved at us and told us in broken English that she would be right there. She was one of Bumbu's daughters. He had at least five that I knew of. I didn't know if she would remember me. She grabbed an order pad and a pen before heading our way. She walked up to us with pen and pad in hand. She looked at me and smiled from ear to ear.

"I member you. You stay here before. You diver."

"Yes and you are one of Bumbu's daughters."

"You too remember me!"

She was delighted that I remembered her.

"Is your father here?"

"Yes, he's in kitchen. I get him. You wait."

She hurried through the old west looking double doors to the kitchen. I could hear her speaking quickly in Balinese then I could hear the unmistakable voice of Bumbu.

The short and stocky Indonesian pushed open the swinging doors.

"Rousser?"

For some reason everyone here called me Rousser, except for Coke.

"It is you!"

"Hello Bumbu."

He gave me a huge bear hug and I thought he was going to break my spine.

"So good to see you."

He looked at Addison and looked back at me.

"Who this?"

"This is Addison."

"I am Bumbu. This is my place."

"You his woman?"

"Yes. I am."

"So sorry to hear that. You can do better next time."

"Enough, Bumbu. How have you been? How's the business going?"

"I'm good. Need help for restaurant and bar. Another daughter married. Now an employee short."

"I'm sorry for you but happy for your daughter."

"Sit down. Relax. You want coffee?"

"Of course."

He yelled something in Balinese to his daughter in the kitchen and she brought out two cups of coffee for Addison and me.

"Thank you, ma'am."

"Such manners from this one. You must be good influence."

"Bumbu, where's Coke?"

The smile left his face.

"You not know?"

"Know what? What's wrong?"

Bumbu sat down at our table in the chair next to me. I had never seen him sitting. He was always running around the restaurant, in and out of the kitchen and mixing drinks behind the bar. He put his hand on my shoulder.

"Coke is gone."

"Gone where?"

"He is sleeping."

"He's sleeping?"

"Yes."

I stared at him very confused. Then it hit me. Coke was dead.

In Balinese culture, when someone dies they are said to be asleep. No tears are to be shed. The deceased are only considered temporarily absent and will be reincarnated or journey to Moksha. Moksha is the final resting place that frees spirits from the reincarnation and death cycle.

"When?"

"Two days ago."

"Is he still sleeping?"

"Yes."

"Where is he sleeping?"

"He is in the chapel."

"Can we see him?"

"Of course. I take you."

He yelled something in Balinese to his daughter and we walked out into the street. I stood still for a moment trying to think straight. I never would have expected this. Coke wasn't that old. He was in great shape. He was an Ironman, the Ironman once. How could he be dead? Bumbu met us in the street.

"How, Bumbu?"

"The doctor came down from mountain. Said it was his heart. That is why he is asleep."

Bumbu took us to the chapel. He motioned for us to go inside then left us. I looked at Addison. She looked at me as though I was about to have a meltdown at any moment. I didn't know how I was going to react either. I grabbed her hand and with the other hand I opened the door. I stepped inside. Addison followed close behind me.

The windows were open and a light breeze was flowing through the small room. That's all it was, a small room. He was lying on two tables pushed end to end in the middle of the room. Evidently the existing ceremonial table was not long enough for his long frame. They had to improvise. He wasn't laid out straight as one would expect to see the departed at a viewing in the States. In Bali, the body is positioned as if the person was actually sleeping. He was lying on his side with his arms bent towards him. His hands were joined as if praying. His knees were slightly bent as if he were in a relaxed fetal position. A thin pad was underneath him and a gold pillow was under his head. A white sheet with gold trim was draped over him. He looked like he was sleeping.

"I'm sorry Rick."

"It's OK. No. It's not OK. I wanted... I just wanted to see him...so he could see I was OK and turned my life around...that I wasn't a complete screw up."

"Rick. Stop."

"Dr. Biterman and now him. My father, the man who used to be my grandfather, Dr. Biterman and Coke were the most important men in my life. The men I looked up to and respected. They each had traits I tried to emulate. Each was special in his own way. I lost Dr. Biterman then I lost my grandfather and now him. My father is the only one left."

"He does look like he is sleeping."

"Yes. He does. It's strange but that makes me feel better. The cremation should be tomorrow. It is usually done three days after a person dies. Goodbye Coke. Thank you. Thank you for believing in me when I didn't."

I broke down as I walked outside. I lowered my head so Addison wouldn't see me crying and I leaned against the front of the chapel. Addison turned me towards her and hugged me tightly. I couldn't stop crying. Addison began crying.

"Why are you crying?"

"Because you are and I love you."

"I don't ever want to make you cry. I'll stop if you will."

"OK."

"Do you mind if I see him alone?"

"Of course not."

"Thank you."

I went back inside and slowly walked over to Coke. I thought about what brought me to this place and what brought me back to this place. I had grown a lot as a person. I matured and accepted the good and bad in life. But, just because I accepted the bad didn't mean I had to like it. We all die. That's part of it. It's ironic. You have to live to die.

Coke lived. I wished he lived long enough for me to see him again. But, he didn't. I accepted that. At least, I could see him leave this world. I didn't miss that at least. I placed my hand on top of his and choked back the tears.

"Goodbye Coke."

I stepped outside and found Addison waiting for me. I smiled at her while still trying to hold back the tears. She gave me a hug.

"Let's find Bumbu. He can get us a room for tonight."

"If he can't, I'd rather take my chances sleeping on the beach. That car is not very comfortable."

We got back to the restaurant. Our coffees were still there. Bumbu's daughter saw we had returned and brought us two fresh cups.

"Thank you."

"Welcome."

A couple minutes later she brought us some breakfast. I didn't have much of an appetite.

"You need to eat something Rick."

"I know. I'm just not very hungry right now."

"I understand but you did say this was his favorite place for breakfast, right?"

"Is. It is his favorite place for breakfast. Remember, he's only sleeping."

"Yes, excuse me. I forgot he was sleeping."

We finished breakfast and Bumbu came out of the kitchen and directed us to a small hotel along the beach that had been built after Coke bought me a plane ticket and I flew home. It was a nice place, small but tidy. Apparently, two surfers had been kicked out of our new room. I felt bad but not that bad. We unpacked our things and lay down on the bed. I wanted to take a nap but couldn't sleep, neither could Addison.

"Let's go to the beach."

"OK. You feel up to it?"

"Yeah, I'm good."

"Put on your swimsuit and I'll unpack our stuff."

Addison went to the bathroom to change. I pulled my old board shorts out of my suitcase. I had worn them in Hawaii, Tahiti, and Bali. I was wearing them the morning Coke found me passed out on the beach only feet away from drowning. They were very faded and threads were coming loose. They were stretched out at the waist and I had to pull the drawstring tight or they would fall right off me.

That happened one time when I was helping Coke unload tanks off the boat. Coke handed me one of the tanks when the drawstring came loose and my swimsuit dropped to my ankles. I dropped the tank in a rush to pull up my swimsuit and it landed on my right foot. I pulled up my swimsuit but when the pain registered I instinctively reached for my foot and my swimsuit fell down again. I fell on the dock and wriggled myself back into my swimsuit and pulled the drawstring very tight. I sat up to check on my foot hoping I hadn't broken any bones. Coke was laughing so hard he almost fell off the boat into the water. I didn't think it was so funny.

Addison and I walked to the beach carrying our masks, snorkels and fins. It was a sunny day and the water was calm so visibility was awesome. We saw an assortment of beautiful fish swimming around the coral reef and a green eel even stuck his head out to greet us. We finished snorkeling and sat on the beach to rest.

"I wish I had something better to wear tomorrow. I didn't know I was coming to a cremation ceremony."

"I'm glad to see you joking again. You worried me this morning."

"It was a disappointing morning. Let's go back to the room and get cleaned up."

We showered and lay down on the bed. We both fell asleep and didn't wake up until the next morning.

In fact, we almost missed the ceremony. We arrived at the chapel just before the Ngaben, or cremation ceremony, was about to begin. Even if we had arrived late, I'm sure Bumbu would have made everyone wait for us.

Coke's body was placed into a simple wooden coffin, just barely though. No one had thought about the coffin being too small for him. The coffin was placed inside a sarcophagus resembling a Lembu. Lembu is the Balinese word for water buffalo. Coke's water buffalo was made out of papier-mache and wood. It was painted and looked like a real golden haired water buffalo. The local artisans did a very good job.

The men of Kuta lifted the sarcophagus and carried it toward the beach in a zig-zag pattern. This is done to confuse evil spirits and keep them away from the departed. We and the townspeople followed them as confused tourists looked on. The sarcophagus was placed a few feet away from the water's edge. The burning of the sarcophagus is the climax of the Ngaben. I asked Bumbu if I could do something before the fire was started.

Well, actually I first asked him why he didn't just have all of his daughters carry Coke to the beach. He gave me the stink eye. He didn't think it was funny. I did.

I walked up to the water buffalo. It suddenly occurred to me that he was sleeping as well. That made me smile. I hung my medal on his horn. The ribbon slid down his horn and the medal rest upon his cheek.

"Take good care of him handsome sleeping Lembu."

I stepped back and walked to Addison. Everyone gathered in a semi-circle around the Lembu sleeping on the beach. Bumbu carried the lit torch to Coke's enshrined body and threw it under the chest of the magnificent beast.

Those Balinese don't fool around when it comes to cremations because that thing exploded into a fireball sending a mushroom cloud high into the air. It was like Hiroshima on the beach. Everyone ran away from it as fast as they could possibly run in the sand. I checked to make sure my eyebrows weren't singed off.

When the bonfire/funeral pyre died down, the townspeople left. Bumbu was the last to go. He hugged Addison and me before returning to town. I was so grateful I could be here to say farewell and see Coke leave this world.

We returned the next morning to gather ashes. There were still some hot coals. The Balinese sure know how to cremate. They've got it down to a science. Some of the ashes had been washed away by the ocean and some had been carried away by the trade winds. It was impossible to tell which ashes were water buffalo or Coke.

We gathered what we could in a ceremonial container that Bumbu had given to us. I sifted through the ashes hoping I wouldn't touch one of the hot coals. I found it just under the ashes where it once hung from a water buffalo's horn. The ribbon was now part of the ashes but the medal was intact. I washed it off and put it in my pocket.

We took the ashes with us and boarded Coke's boat. I took us out to Coke's favorite dive spot and killed the engine. I gave Addison a kiss and took the container from her. I didn't say anything. I just poured his ashes into the water being careful not to have a *Big Lebowski* moment. I took the medal out of my pocket and dropped it into the water.

"Was that your medal?"

"Yes."

"Why did you do that?"

"It being here means more to me than framing it or hanging it on a wall at home."

Addison and I stayed in Kuta. I taught her how to dive and we even took some tourists diving to help fund our stay. We stayed in the back of the dive shop. The small cot in the back didn't bother Addison. It ensured I had to snuggle her every night. I didn't want to stay at Coke's house. It would have been too awkward. Bumbu said it was an acceptable practice but I still didn't want to. Addison fell in love with Kuta. She didn't want to leave.

"You need to finish pharmacy school."

"Forget pharmacy school. I want to stay here."

"Forget pharmacy school? What are you talking about? You started something, something important, and you need to finish it."

"I want to stay here though."

"Listen, after you graduate, if you want to come back we can. We can make a life here if that's what you still want to do. OK?"

"You promise?"

"I promise."

Then we kissed.